TERRY SILVERMAN AND THE DEMON WOLF

Terry Silverman and the Demon Wolf

Copyright © 2020 by Sikandar Vayani

Cover art and map by Jennifer Birgersson

Seal of the Khizaar illustration by Zainab Vayani

For more info visit: www.spellcraftpress.com

First published in the United Kingdom
Thank you for buying an official copy of this book and
for complying with copyright laws

ISBN: 978-1-8381505-8-7

First Edition: 2020

10 9 8 7 6 5 4 3 2 1

TERRY SILVERMAN AND THE DEMON WOLF

SIKANDAR VAYANI

SPELLCRAFT PRESS

Contents

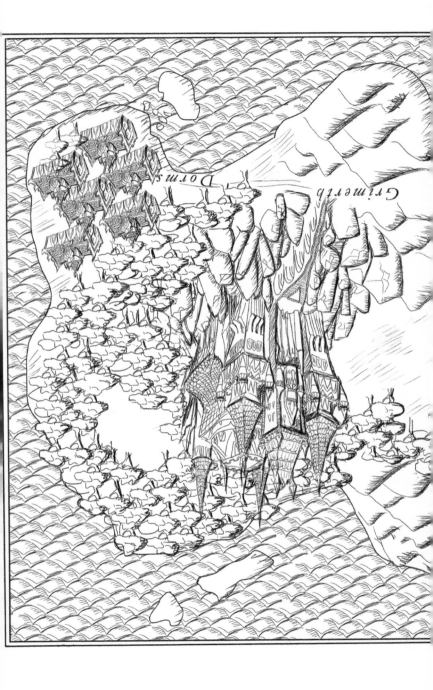

1

Through the Sealed Door

There exists a realm where the light of day cannot reach and the creatures of the night speak; a place of mystery and wonder, of magic and horror, and peculiar amusement. A place you only hear stories about. A place that exists somewhere far, far away and yet so close, you can step inside within an instant. It's right before your very eyes, and yet you're blind, but rest assured, you may find it in time.

This is the story of Terry Silverman, and like any other story, this journey begins in the most magical place in the world: the airport.

Dressed in a dark red blazer and black shirt, young Terry tapped his feet anxiously in the departure lounge as his eyes surveyed his surroundings. He was searching for signs of the extraordinary. Perhaps a walking, talking skeleton? His eyes flicked back and forth. No, none of them around. Maybe a zombie instead? He scratched his head, trying to think. Ah, but wait, they only lurked around cemeteries eating dead people, so they couldn't be here. Maybe a ghost, then? Yes, he thought, a ghost most definitely should be here. Surely one would pop up from the ground below at any moment, or maybe through that wall on the left. But, no. Nothing! So, then, where was everybody hiding?

It was midday on one of the hottest days of the year. Terry had been slurping on the last of his carton of tomato juice, and no matter how much he looked, he just couldn't find any other Grimerth students like himself. Strange, his uncle had told him that if he waited here, he would see them, but that was over four hours ago, so why hadn't anybody shown up?

For so long, Terry had been waiting for a chance to meet others like him. You see, Terry Silverman had a secret that no one else knew about. He was a vampire, but not just any vampire—a day-walking vampire. What was the difference? Well, for one, he was able to sit in the sun and not burn to death. For another, his skin was much more tanned than the usual pale-skinned variety, and he could see his own reflection in the mirror. He was also a vegetarian and substituted blood with tomato juice. Both tasted horrible, but it was desperately required for his nutritional needs.

Of course, being a vampire had its shortcomings too. One of the biggest was that it made human friendships incredibly problematic, especially for someone like Terry with small sharp fangs and piercing red eyes. Most humans were too frightened to be anywhere near him and thought he was a weirdo because of his looks. He'd spent thirteen miserable years as a loner, unable to connect with others and being called a freak.

Terry had no family either, his parents died long before he could remember. The only person remotely close to Terry was his uncle, but his busy work schedule meant he was hardly ever around for the boy, leaving Terry all by himself.

But now things were different! Now he was joining Grimerth, a school for monsters and other ghastly creatures, just like him. He couldn't wait! Except there was still no one here from the undead ghoulish world.

Terry sighed. Had he missed them somehow? Everyone and everything he saw looked so normal. An impatient middle-aged businessman holding a briefcase and checking his watch repeatedly, an unruly family of eight running to their gate because they were late for their flight, and an old man who sat down next to Terry holding up a newspaper. The headline advertised another mysterious disappearance near Fairhedge, Terry's hometown in West London.

"Terry Silverman?" said a voice. A young girl with blue eyes and dark blue hair wearing a cape and sporting a witch's hat suddenly popped up beside him. She appeared to be about thirteen, the same age as Terry, perhaps a year or two older. In her hand was a clipboard, and she had a pen tucked behind her ear.

Terry eyed her with caution.

"Right, I suppose I should introduce myself," she said, scratching the back of her head. "My name's Almira Khizaar. I'm here to guide you to your flight for Occulomundus."

"You're a student?"

"Yes, but I'm also a prefect, which means sometimes the teachers like to assign me work. They call it personal development. I call it child labour."

"Where's your broomstick?" Terry asked.

"In the closet. Do you have your ticket?" she said, getting straight to business.

Not a lot of fun this one, he thought. Terry rummaged through his backpack and handed his ticket to her.

"How did you know who I was?" he asked. "I don't exactly have a name tag."

Almira looked at him with a blank expression as she took the ticket from him and examined it carefully. "You mean, besides the obvious fact that you have red eyes?"

"Ah," he said, "how silly of me. Suppose that does give it away. Guess I'm just used to people thinking that it's coloured contact lenses."

"And then there's your shoes as well," said Almira, still studying the ticket.

"My shoes?" questioned Terry, looking down curiously.

"There's some rare Peruvian soil on the soles," she said, passing Terry back his ticket.

Terry arched an eyebrow. "How would you know it's Peruvian?" he asked. "And how can you possibly see the soles?"

"I can't. I'm just making stuff up. They do look quite worn though, especially considering those shoes came out only last week."

"Well, we vampires are quick on our feet," said Terry. "Or so I hear. I've actually never met another vampire, but I know I'm pretty fast."

"How very modest. See here, I have the class roster," she said, holding up her clipboard to reveal a collection of passport style photos with the names of each student beneath them.

Terry stared at her with a blank expression. "Couldn't you have just said that from the start?" he asked.

Almira smiled. "Now where would the fun be in that?"

Okay, he considered, maybe she was a little entertaining.

"Well, now that we've cleared that up, come this way so I can finally be done with this."

He followed behind her, keeping an eye out for the others. "Where are the rest?" he asked.

"They've already boarded," said Almira. "You're the last one."

Terry stopped, dumbfounded. He'd been here for hours! How could he possibly be the last one? He hurried after her. "But there's been no announcements to board!" he cried.

Almira turned to face him with a supercilious gaze. "Come on now, do you really think that a flight to a hidden supernatural island is going to be announced to the public?"

Terry's face went red. Stupid, stupid, stupid. He should have known the United Government of Monsters— otherwise known as UGOM—would want to keep things hush hush. He'd heard from his uncle how secretive UGOM were, so secretive in fact, that only very few high profile human beings, like the Prime Minister or the Queen of England herself, knew about them. Everyday folk had no idea. They would just go about their days blissfully unaware about the truth of the supernatural. And here Terry had the audacity to think that UGOM would allow their hidden world to be announced in a public airport. How foolish of him!

Terry pulled out his inhaler from his trouser pocket and held it to his lips, taking a deep puff to calm himself. Maybe it would be better to stay silent and simply observe. He followed her to a door in a quiet corner of the lounge that read AUTHORISED PERSONNEL ONLY.

She waved her index finger at the doorknob in a circular motion. "Take the hand outstretched before you," she whispered, her words sounding like a spell. "Forever, together, we'll take a journey." Her voice was soft and calming. "My heart surrenders. This isn't the world I know, but I'll step through the dark door. And I'll find myself in a distant realm of dream-like logic. Lost in its own time and reality. A world of magic and monsters."

There was a faint yellow glow that emitted momentarily from the doorknob. Immediately the sound of locks turning could be heard, followed by a strange hiss as the door slid open.

15

It was pitch black inside, but the witch entered without any hesitation. Terry checked his surroundings, not a single person was paying attention. He stared into the void before him, his throat tightening. Despite being a vampire, he wasn't used to the darkness. He'd spent most of his time in daylight, so his eyes hadn't adjusted to the night like normal vampires.

"What's the hold up?" Almira's voice echoed from the vacuum of emptiness.

"Just a moment," Terry replied, taking a deep breath. Okay. One. Two. Three.

Eyes closed, he stepped forward and held out his hands to avoid bumping into anything. A long time passed. He dared to open his eyes and look ahead, but it was so dark that he couldn't tell left from right. How much further was it? He continued in a straight line with his arms still outstretched. After a few moments, he could see a bright light. He ran towards it and found himself in what appeared to be, for the most part, the same airport—only he could see through the windows that it was dark outside and filled with both humans and monsters.

A group of bespectacled werewolves carried backpacks while walking in a pack, their noses buried in books. Not far from them were a few zombies repeatedly singing about eating brains. They were quickly pushed aside by an

Egyptian mummy, his bandages unravelling as he tried to make off with stolen toilet paper. A couple of large, ugly ogres with batons in hand were in hot pursuit.

Ah, finally the bizarre! Terry couldn't help but smile; this was just what he'd been hoping for.

2

The Skeleton

"Stop gawking," said Almira. "We don't have a lot of time."

"Right. Sorry," said Terry. He continued to trail behind her.

Once they arrived at the gate, he showed his boarding pass to the goblin at the counter. The goblin was a huge, unpleasant creature with putrid breath, wrinkled green skin, and big pointy ears. He checked Terry's ticket without batting an eye and grumpily gestured for him to board the plane. Such a jolly fellow, Terry thought.

Inside, there were three creatures on each side of the aisle. On the left-hand side were all the girls, and to the right, all the boys. Almira sat down at the front. "Your seat is much further back," she said. "You'll be with the other first years. Now shoo." She made a sweeping gesture with her hand to show that she wanted rid of him.

Terry made his way along the narrow aisle, but once he'd got to his assigned seat, he found that a snotty nosed vampire boy wearing a black cape with an upturned collar was sitting in his seat.

Ugh, there always had to be one fancy looking idiot. The boy had a smug look on his face that told Terry he thought the world of himself. He appeared to be trying to chat up the pretty girl sitting in the seat on the other side, but she seemed entirely uninterested.

"You're in my seat," said Terry, squeezing between the two of them.

The boy didn't take too kindly to the interruption. "What's your problem?" he said in a plummy voice. He stood up, bringing himself face-to-face with Terry, and bared his fangs at him.

Maybe this wasn't such a bright idea. Only now did it dawn on Terry that he was picking a fight with a fully-fledged bloodsucking vampire. He was also acutely aware of the possibility that he may be starting a scene and creating unnecessary attention for himself. But wait, why should he be scared? Terry was a vampire too, and not just any vampire, he was a vampire who could walk in broad daylight and not get burnt to a crisp by doing so. In this battle between fang-bearers, he had the high ground. Terry tried his best not to move, maintaining a steady gaze.

"Well?" said the smug boy.

"I said you're in my seat," he repeated. "That's the problem."

"I don't see your name on it."

"No, but it has my ticket number on it." Terry's confidence was rising. He was on a roll. "Or can't you count, you blockhead?"

Okay, so maybe the last part wasn't really necessary, and *blockhead*? Really? Great choice of words, Terry. But someone had to tell the kid or else he'd never learn.

Some of the surrounding students started to take an interest. The smug boy clenched his fist, looking like he was ready to hit Terry, but before he could say or do anything more, a minotaur in a fitted blue suit and red bow tie raised his head from a seat in the front row.

"Ahem! And what, may I ask, is going on here?" said the minotaur with a loud, authoritative voice that drew everybody's attention.

"It's Tompkins, the deputy headmaster," whispered one of the male students covered in silvery fish-like scales.

"I heard he tamed a basilisk with just a glare," said a tall female elf with light blue skin and dark blonde hair.

"I heard he killed an ogre with his bare hands," said the twin elf sitting next to her.

Tompkins got out of his seat and strode towards Terry and the smug boy, steam exhaling from his long snout. He had a human body, but his eyes inside his bullish head were small white slits with no pupils, nor irises, giving the impression of a soulless being. "Ah Kurt, I should have known," he said, addressing the smug boy first. "I would think that you'd know better now that you're joining intermediary school."

"Sorry, sir, we just had a small misunderstanding," said Kurt, bowing his head slightly.

"And you are?" asked Tompkins as he turned to Terry.

Terry gave a small, courteous bow by placing his right hand across his chest and nodding his head briefly before introducing himself. "Terry Silverman."

Tompkins studied him for a moment, rubbing his chin thoughtfully. "Hmm," said the minotaur, "I don't recall seeing you at Grimerth Foundation School."

Terry lowered his right hand. "I'm a new student, sir," he explained. "I've only attended human schools prior to today."

"That must be why I don't recognise you. So, Terry, can you tell me what happened?"

"He's in my seat," said Terry. "I asked him to move and he refused."

"Like I said, there was a misunderstanding, sir. I was just making my way to my seat. I apologise," said Kurt. "I'll be going now." He turned, and as he did, he shoved Terry, pushing him backwards against the vampire girl's seat. "Oops, sorry about that," said Kurt.

Terry picked himself up off the floor. "You did that on purpose!"

"Ahem," said Tompkins, ensuring that both of them didn't forget his presence.

Kurt eyed Terry, but he said nothing more as he headed to his own seat, much further back.

"Well then, Terry, please, make yourself comfortable," said Tompkins.

"Thank you, sir." Terry nodded his head and sat down in his seat. He watched Tompkins head towards the front, past the drawn curtains and into the teacher's section.

"Well that was interesting," said a meek voice sitting next to Terry. Terry turned and was taken aback by what he saw next, so much so that he almost fell off his seat with his jaw dropped in shock. The hooded cloak and downturned head had kept this person hidden earlier, but now Terry could see clearly. It was a skeleton! A real live talking skeleton! They really existed!

Of course, none of the other students around him paid the least bit of attention. The werewolf at the window seat was completely ignoring the fact that there was a talking pile of bones next to him. And why should he care anyway? For this werewolf, seeing a skeleton was probably just a normal everyday occurrence, nothing at all of interest. He was entirely immersed in his own little world, holding a mirror up to his face in one hand and busy plucking hairs off his bushy face with a tweezer in the other hand.

"They call me Fergus Gravestone," said the skeleton, removing his hood and revealing his bony skull. He held out a bony hand. "How do you do? Me? Well, can't complain. Least I'm still alive. No, wait. That's not quite right is it?"

Terry chuckled in disbelief. "You're weird … I like it." There was a certain splendour for him in seeing the unnatural after living life amongst mundane normality. He held out his hand with long pointed nails, clasped Fergus's bony fingers, and introduced himself.

The skeleton rattled, leaning in close, a little too close. His empty eye sockets peered deep into Terry's soul. "So, you're not from around here."

"Well, yes, I did just say that to the scary looking teacher."

He pulled back. "Fascinating. So, you're new. Well, I'll be damned. No wait, I already am. Long story though, you probably don't want to hear it. Say, you look like the kind of person that likes to play games. Do you want to play a game?" he asked as he pulled out a deck of trading cards from inside his cloak and began shuffling them like an expert. "These cards are based on famous monsters," he explained. "Before, it was only possible to get them in packs of gum, but then they realised they could sell the cards for more without the gum. Personally, I wasn't happy about that. It completely killed my allowance. I hardly have enough money left for food now. Lucky for me, school meals are free."

Once the plane had taken off, Fergus began setting up the cards on the table tray in front of the seat and explained the rules and strategy behind the game to Terry, going into a lot of detail. Lots and lots of detail. So much so that Terry's head was starting to hurt. Once the second game was over, Terry tried changing the subject.

"So, you're a skeleton?"

"I am? Hell's bells and buckets of blood! Does this mean I died, or was I born like this?"

"Which is it?"

"Good question. I'll let you know when I know."

A tall zombie with high heels, unsightly frizzy red hair, and a crimson stewardess outfit tapped Terry on the shoulder. She offered him a newspaper to read. He glanced at the paper and dismissed it with a wave. She then offered it to Fergus who also rejected it. The werewolf at the end ignored her entirely, still too busy plucking his never-ending facial hairs.

"It's always the same stuff," said the skeleton. "The Demon Wolf strikes again. Another missing monster found washed ashore, mutilated body of course. The usual speeches from UGOM about the safety of Grimerth and their promise to protect us and all that rubbish."

"Demon Wolf?" asked Terry.

"Ah, they call him that 'cause all the victims look like they transformed into some sort of demonic wolf before being completely ripped apart and destroyed."

Terry cocked his head. "I didn't know monsters could transform into other monsters. How does it work exactly?"

"How does what work?"

"Say if a mummy gets bitten by a werewolf, does it transform into a wolf mummy?"

"Nonsense," Fergus snorted. "Werewolf bites kill, they don't transform you into a werewolf. That's just stuff humans made up. We get their movies and books imported here, you know, hilarious stuff. Always gives us a good laugh."

"So then, how do humans become werewolves?"

Fergus shrugged his bones. "Don't look at me, I'm no teacher." He checked his surroundings and started fanning himself with his left hand. "My, oh my, is it me, or is it getting hot in here?" He pulled off his purple cloak, rattling his naked skeleton body. "Ah, much better."

The decaying stewardess returned with a cart to serve lunch which contained packets of crisps, sandwiches, chocolates, and packaged ready meals. Thank God it was normal food, Terry was starved. One thing he'd been concerned about before coming to the island was the sustenance that would be provided. For some reason, he was under the impression he would get something he'd be unable to eat, like boiled spiders or mashed bats, or something stupid like that. He grabbed his spoon and dug into a pot of rice. Eww, the rice was cold. Was airplane food always bad, no matter where you went?

"What would you like to drink?" asked the stewardess.

"Milk please," said Fergus. He then whispered to Terry, "I need to strengthen me bones."

"Tomato juice for me, please," said Terry.

She poured their drinks, handed the plastic cups to them both, and then turned to the girls' side. Terry's eyes fell on the girl that Kurt had pushed him into earlier. She wore a black dress and had long silky black hair, pale skin, fiery-red eyes, and the smallest, cutest fangs that rested on her plump bottom lip when she opened her mouth.

"Who's that vampire girl?" asked Terry.

"Forget it, Emmy's way out of your league," said the skeleton. "You're probably better off going after a nerdy elf. Actually, on second thought," he said, rubbing his chin thoughtfully while studying Terry's face. He then put a bony hand on Terry's shoulder as if to show sympathy for him. "My condolences. Perhaps you should give up now or go for someone blind."

"Are you calling me ugly?" said Terry.

"Not at all. You're very handsome," said Fergus.

Terry couldn't tell if the skeleton was being serious or joking. His lack of facial expressions made it difficult to deduce.

"Whatever," said Terry dismissively, turning his attention back to the vampire girl. For some reason, she now had a clothing peg on her nose. Then he realised the reason: there was garlic bread on her tray.

Her eyes began to water as she drew the garlic bread near to her mouth. She closed her eyes and took a deep bite, her features twisted with pain. "It burns!" she cried through her mouthful of food, lips smacking together noisily. "Ugh, but it tastes so good! Pain is pleasure." She went for another bite, her face twisting again, but that didn't deter her from her meal.

Terry wasn't sure whether or not he should be concerned for her. "You love garlic bread so much you're willing to die for it?" he asked.

Emmy stared at him blankly and spoke while still chewing. "Well, I'd be lying if I said it didn't hurt. But to be honest, I think I'm building up resistance towards it." She pounded her chest with a fist after she'd finished and sighed, leaning back in her seat with closed eyes. "Oh my God, the way the buttery garlic just melts in your mouth is simply amazing."

"I told you she's weird," whispered Fergus.

"When did you say that?"

"Like, right now. Weren't you paying attention?" He then turned to his cup of milk and held it up. "Do you like milk?"

"I don't mind it," said Terry.

"Best drink in the seven realms." He took a sip, but since he was nothing more than bones, it passed right through him and straight onto his seat, making it look like he'd wet himself.

Terry cracked up laughing.

"Hey," said Emmy, looking a little annoyed that Terry had turned his attention away from her for a moment. "Are you a day-walker?"

"Sorry?" said Terry, controlling his laughter.

29

"A day-walker," she repeated. "You know, vampires that can walk in daylight. You look like one. Your skin is tanned, so I'm guessing you spend a lot of time in the sun. It's rare to see a day-walker round here."

"How come?"

"Well 'cause we're both awake at different times."

"Oh yeah."

"Obvious much?"

Terry didn't respond, continuing to sip his tomato juice.

"So, what's it like?" she said, staring at him as if to study his features.

"What's what like?"

"Duh, to walk in the sunlight?" she said impatiently.

"Oh right," said Terry. "It's umm, bright."

"You're so lucky," she said, turning her gaze away and looking towards the closed window shade. "It always looks so beautiful in pictures. Clear blue skies and the light of day. Just for once, I wish I could see it for real. Take a walk with the hot wind in my face and the warm rays of the sun against my skin. Ah, but I guess it's just a dream for me. An impossible dream."

3

School for Monsters

After the plane landed, they had to travel by boat to the mainland of Occulomundus. From there, they boarded a bus. Most of the journey had been covered by thick fog which only began to clear once they passed a small town and approached the school grounds. As they did, the castle loomed into view. It was a towering behemoth that stood silhouetted against the night sky in the pale moonlight, strangely menacing in its gothic silence. The lights illuminating the windows gave the castle a lifelike feel, adding to the foreboding sense that it may be alive and staring right back at them. Here it was, the other world, one far removed from the reality Terry had known and grown accustomed to.

Upon closer inspection, he noticed that above the castle, high in the sky, protruding out from the clouds was the inverted head of a decrepit old grey building, completely separate to the castle. What an irregular choice of location! It looked as though it may crumble and fall upon the castle below at any moment.

"Why is there an upside-down building floating in the sky?" asked Terry.

"That's where UGOM headquarters is," said Fergus. "Also known as GITS."

"GITS?" said Terry, arching an eyebrow.

"The 'Government in the Sky', of course," he explained as if it were the most obvious answer in the world.

"Of course," said Terry, looking back up. "How do you get up there anyway?"

"Don't look at me. I've never seen anyone go up or down that thing. Although I've heard a rumour that there's an invisible ladder you're supposed to climb, but if you ask me, that just sounds like a lot of nonsense."

Everyone fell silent as they exited the bus, which stopped outside a long set of steep stone steps that led up to the castle. There must have been around one hundred, maybe more. And dear God, it was a lengthy climb, taking nearly thirty minutes to reach the top. Some students were left gasping for breath, and Terry was craving a large glass of tomato juice to quench his thirst.

Tompkins was at the front, the only teacher in sight, completely unfazed by the journey. Before him was a huge, double-panelled black door with ugly gargoyles perched each side on ledges. They looked like they were made of stone until one of them winked at Terry, and he nearly jumped out of his skin.

Tompkins knocked on the entrance three times, and after a few moments, the doors creaked wide open, but there was nobody on the other side, only a large hall that seemed to be covered in a swirling mist. Tompkins nodded his head, almost as if he were greeting someone.

Terry wondered if perhaps the minotaur had gone mad because now it looked as if Tompkins was talking to himself, making light conversation.

"It was a pleasant journey, thank you for asking. Ah yes, indeed. Yes, of course. And a good night to you too, sir!" said Tompkins before continuing into the castle.

Everyone else followed closely behind in a long line, mumbling and exchanging confused glances with each other.

Once inside, it was surprisingly warm and welcoming, the vast entrance now lit with flaming torches that floated in mid-air. On the floor, painted in golden brown colours, was the school's coat of arms. It consisted of a lady vampire on one side and a werewolf on the other. A demonic skull rested between them, and on the banderole around the base was the school's name: GRIMERTH SCHOOL FOR MONSTERS AND OTHER GHASTLY CREATURES. At the far end was a reception desk, and stationed there was a tall, slim, purple-skinned gorgon wearing coke-bottle glasses and dressed like a nanny, her snake hair covered by a scarf. Leading behind the desk was the entrance to what appeared to be a courtyard where some other students had already gathered.

Tompkins guided them to another set of stairs to the left of the reception. "All your luggage will be delivered to your rooms," he explained as they began to climb to the top. "Your classes will take place at night, and you'll be sleeping during the day. I shall be taking you all to the assembly hall, where the headmistress, Mrs. Alexa Autumn, will give her welcome speech."

Mounted on the walls were portraits of famous monsters throughout history. Terry recognised a few from the card game he'd played with Fergus on the plane. There was Countess Luna of Leo, a thousand-year-old witch with wrinkly green skin, curly white hair, and a crooked nose who had learned the secret of immortality at the cost of her sanity. She was a far cry from Almira, the pale young witch with blue eyes and dark blue hair that Terry had met earlier.

Next up was General Flexiback, a grizzly, barrel-chested werewolf with an eye patch. He was a veteran of two wars between the vampires and the werewolves over a hundred years ago.

And then there was Snark Dia, the current head of UGOM who came into power a decade ago. He looked like a normal person with his jet-black hair and pale complexion. Everything about him was a mystery. Nobody knew who he really was nor where he came from, only that he one day appeared and was rather abruptly appointed the head of UGOM by the previous Prime President. He was rarely seen by the public and often had his right-hand man, Hans Coil, do his work for him.

"After the assembly you shall all be free to do as you wish," said Tompkins, coming to a stop just outside an old wooden door. "If you find yourself famished, you may go to the dining room where we have an all-night buffet open to everyone. Or, if you prefer something lighter, then please feel free to use one of our many vending machines you'll find located throughout the castle. You may freely roam the first twelve floors in any of the towers, but I ask that you refrain from venturing onto the thirteenth and the dungeons below. If you wish to head to the dorm rooms and relax, remember to check-out at the reception desk before you do so."

Tompkins opened the door that led into the assembly hall which featured a colossal stage at the front and rows and rows of seats that inclined upwards, similar to being at a theatre. He gestured the students to sit down and made his way to the front stage.

"Ahem! Fellow monsters, if I could have your attention please," said Tompkins, once all the students had been seated. "It is my great pleasure for me to introduce your headmistress—although she has no head—please welcome Mrs. Alexa Autumn."

In the silence, the approaching sound of loud click-clacking footsteps echoed, and moments later, a headless woman dressed in business attire walked in through the entrance. She positioned herself at the stand, held up her papers to read, and then said nothing.

Everyone remained silent as they fidgeted in their seats. In fact, nobody said anything for a lengthy and awkward amount of time. Finally, Tompkins broke the silence. "The headmistress says that she would like to thank me, the deputy headmaster, or as many of you know my name, Mr.

Basil Tompkins, for my lovely introduction, and take this opportunity to welcome you all to Grimerth, School for Monsters and Other Ghastly Creatures."

How Tompkins understood what the headless woman wanted to say was beyond Terry's comprehension. She made no gestures with her hands nor showed any body language that could be interpreted. It was impossible to tell if she was even speaking, let alone what she was saying. Yet Tompkins continued to interpret as if he were able to fully comprehend her every word, perhaps through telepathy. It was the most peculiar welcome assembly Terry had ever attended.

"It is often said that our greatest fear is the light," said Tompkins. "Our light. We fear our greatest selves, but the brave amongst us, the truly brave, bathe in the light that they create. It is our aim here at Grimerth to enrich your lives and bring you each one step closer to your greatest self. Some of you have joined us from our foundation school, while others have come from outside schools, including those from the human realm. We welcome all of you to Grimerth equally and hope that you will enjoy your time here.

"There are four houses that you have been grouped into. You'll know the details of which you've been assigned to tomorrow night. We have House Arsalan, in honour of the hero who saved us and the greatest spellcaster to have ever lived. House Barodas, so that we may never forget the Jackal King who once threatened us and the seven realms. And finally, House Carmilla and House Diane, a tribute to the founders of Grimerth."

After explaining the houses, Tompkins went on to talk about the facilities available at Grimerth, like a new library that was being built underground and would be ready by January. There was also talk about a university programme that had just been put in place for those who wished to pursue higher education after graduating from advanced school. For Terry that decision was still five years away. He had to complete intermediary school before going on to advanced and thinking about university. Then there was talk about the classes they would be taking this year, followed by some concerns that had been raised by parents regarding the Demon Wolf incidents and how measures were being taken to protect the school.

Terry yawned. If he hadn't been so tired, he would have been interested in listening to more of the speech, but as it stood, he'd had no sleep since he had packed his bags in the early hours of the morning. It was now two hours past midnight, and he was ready to hit the hay.

After the assembly, Terry and Fergus headed to the dorms, which were located just outside the castle and towards the edge of the island where they had a view of the ocean and the thick fog hanging over it.

It turned out Terry and Fergus would be sharing a room together. The room itself was rather spacious and well-lit, equipped with a mini fridge, bunk bed, study desks, a fitted closet, and a small bathroom.

"Dibs on the closet," said Fergus, throwing his purple hood onto the floor and rushing inside the open closet, closing it, and then almost immediately snoring.

Terry closed his eyes and pinched the bridge of his nose. Don't question it, he told himself. He didn't want to think about how a skeleton could be snoring. Skeletons shouldn't be talking in the first place anyway, but here was proof of the opposite, and it was exactly what he had been hoping for, weirdos just like him. But right now he just wanted to rest. He didn't bother with changing his clothes or taking a shower, he just slipped off his shoes and curled into the bottom bunk. He could still hear the skeleton in the closet snoring, but he didn't care. Soon he found himself drifting off to sleep.

In his sleep, he dreamt he was flying like a superhero, seeing the island of Occulomundus beneath him. From the castle of Grimerth to a nearby small peaceful town and then towards strange black pyramids on the outskirts of the island. Finally he came to a stop beyond a cemetery near the black pyramids, and he could suddenly hear the dead crying from their graves, the weight of their pain pulling him down. As he fell, an outstretched hand from above grabbed him. He turned to see who had saved him, it was the witch he had met earlier, the one with blue eyes and dark blue hair. She smiled and hauled him up onto her broom. He sat behind her and held tightly onto her as they flew throughout the night, away from the cemetery and towards the stars.

4

Mihai Winter

The next night both Terry and Fergus went to the noticeboards in the hallway on the ground floor to find out which tutor groups they were in. Terry was in House Carmilla. Terry's tutor group, 1HC, also included Fergus and everyone else that had sat in the same row as Terry on the plane, like the pretty vampire girl and the hair plucking werewolf. Before classes officially began, they were instructed to report to Room 108 on the first floor in their tutor groups.

"Please make your way inside," said a voice that seemed to come from nowhere. One by one, all the students entered into the musty old classroom. Terry and Fergus sat at the back on benches at rickety wooden desks. They were supposed to meet their form tutor that night, but he was nowhere to be seen. There was only a disembodied voice.

"Good night, students! I am your form tutor, Mr. C. Reason. The C stands for Clear, but you'll obviously have to call me Mr. Reason. Anyhoo, pleasure to make your acquaintance." His voice was fruity, hyper, and full of life. "Some of you may be wondering where I am. Rest assured, I am standing right here at the front of the class. Now who can answer this riddle for me—what can you hear, but not see?"

"Your voice?" said one of the students.

"That's right, but that's not the answer I wanted, so you're wrong! Ha! The answer I wanted to hear is an invisible form tutor, which is what I am, your invisible form tutor. If you have any problems, please come and see me. No wait, you can't! I'm invisible! Guess you'll never see Clear Reason. Ha-ha! Such a funny man I am. Well, just come to me if you have any troubles, that's what I'm here for, or so I'm told. Now please, let me take the register to ensure that everyone is here. When I say your name, just say 'present' and all will be fine and dandy."

The next teacher they met was just as weird as Reason, but not in a good way. It was a ghost. Miss Robyn Robin was a floating white sheet with black oval eyeholes that taught

Study of the Seven Realms. Apparently, if anyone dared to peek under her sheet, they would die from happiness, because underneath she was so beautiful that it would send the students straight to heaven. To keep everyone in check, she kept floating up and down the class, hovering above their heads and threatening to send them into the afterlife if they misbehaved. It made them all incredibly jumpy and unable to concentrate.

It didn't get any easier after that. Mr. Dimples was a chubby werewolf and the teacher for Curses and Cures, which was an unfortunately long double period that would have otherwise been interesting, had it not been for Mr. Dimples's irregular teaching methods. Whenever a student got a question wrong, he would howl like crazy. He'd then make the student stand up and howl with him for a good five minutes. On the bright side, it did motivate them to pay attention to avoid getting answers wrong and ending up with a sore throat.

For the next lesson, History of Man and Monster, they were taught by Mr. Mihai Winter, a vampire dressed entirely in black. His presence was one that demanded silence and respect, nobody said a word unless they were spoken to. He was tall and well-built. And much like Kurt and Emmy, Mihai Winter had the characteristic pale skin and black hair that nocturnal vampires exhibited. But unlike other vampires, he wore rectangular glasses which slid down his nose from time to time, forcing him to regularly readjust them.

"You can all ignore the 'History of Man' part of this course as you won't be tested on it. I only intend to teach you about our own kind. If you want to learn about humans, feel free to do so in your spare time. If anyone has a problem, then please write a letter to me. Although, I should warn you … your letter may find its way into the trash before I have a chance to read it," he drawled. "The history I will teach you will differ from the history some of you may have learned before. History is one of the more important subjects you will ever study. It is our history that defines who we are and helps shape who we are to become."

He paced up and down. "You see, studying history allows us to understand our past and ideally learn from our mistakes. Unfortunately, even though we are now more civilised than ever, we are still, at our core, ultimately monsters. It is in our nature to fight for survival like any animal, but amongst them all, we are perhaps the worst of creatures. We are greedy, jealous, and highly irrational, which is why we have so many wars and so much suffering."

Winter paused his little ramble and stared out through the window, almost lost in his own thoughts. He then said rather abruptly, "Now can anyone tell me who lives upstairs?"

He scanned the classroom in search of volunteers and immediately froze upon seeing Terry. His brow furrowed into lines, and his eyes narrowed. He seemed to be puzzled, trying to piece something together in his mind. "How very curious. You there," he said finally.

"Yes?" said Terry, alarmed.

"And what is your name, young man?"

"Terry."

"Terry who?"

"Silverman."

"Who was your mother?" Winter's head tilted to one side.

"Sorry?" said Terry.

"Your mother?" Winter repeated.

"I don't know. I never met her. She and my father died when I was a baby," said Terry, feeling confused and wondering if there was a reason why the teacher was randomly asking about his parents.

"My condolences." Winter wandered towards Terry, his long cape dragging along the floor as he did. "Who are your current guardians?"

Now he wanted to know about Terry's uncle? It seemed a very odd question for a teacher to ask a student they'd just met.

"Your guardian?" said Winter impatiently.

"My uncle," answered Terry unintentionally.

"I need his name." Winter leaned in close. His red eyes stared into Terry's own, an unsettling look upon his face.

"Silverman," Terry whispered. "Brian Silverman."

"Is he, by any chance, a werewolf?"

Terry hesitated.

"Well?"

"He's a geneticist and a werewolf ..." Terry's voice trailed off towards the end, but Winter caught the last word, and his eyes lit up.

"I see, I see," said Winter, nodding his head with a raised eyebrow. "A werewolf looking after a vampire. Oh my, how times have changed!"

Several of the other students snickered as if the idea was a very funny one. Terry sank into his chair and pulled out his inhaler from his pocket. What was the deal with this teacher?

"What's this? A vampire with asthma! How very strange!"

"It's for my nerves," Terry explained.

Winter remained still for a moment as if rooted to the spot. "Yes, the resemblance is uncanny," he murmured to himself. He then leaned in closer to Terry, his putrid smelling breath stinking of old blood, and whispered, "I believe I knew your mother, boy."

"Objection!" yelled Fergus, standing up and slamming a bony fist against the table. "You're out of order!" The whole class fell silent. Fergus looked left and right and said, "Huh? Where am I? Was I sleeping again?"

Winter withdrew and straightened up, adjusting his glasses. "Hmm," he said, putting his hands behind his back and returning to the front of the class. "Let me tell you all a little story." He walked towards the windows again and stared out into the night. "Anyone ever heard of the Battle of New Gravespass?" Winter glanced around briefly at the silent students as he waited for a reply. "Nobody? How amusing. Well, let me enlighten you all a little. You see, many, many years ago, there was growing animosity between the Tepes vampires and the Lucien werewolves. Rumours spread that the vampires were building an army to invade and wipe out the werewolves hiding in Jackerwedge." Winter turned back to the class. "And you see, the thing about rumours is that like germs, they spread everywhere."

BRRRRINNG. The school bell sounded loudly.

Winter stopped talking. The class had ended. He eyed Terry and smiled.

"Oh well, until next time then."

5

The Primal Beast

"I'm going to go and see him after our final class tonight," said Terry as he and Fergus made their way to their next class.

"What? Why?"

"When he leaned close to me, he said he knew my mother. I wonder how. I've always wanted to know who she was, but my uncle would never tell me. This could be my chance."

"Want me to come with you?"

"Thanks, but I think I'll go alone for this." Terry's eyes flicked towards Fergus, observing the dull white skeleton walking beside him from skull to toe. "Plus, you make a loud clanking noise wherever you go because of your jiggling bones."

Fergus gasped and mockingly put his bony fingers to his chest. "If I still had a heart, I'd be hurt by that remark."

"Sorry," said Terry, feeling a little guilty. "We only just met, so I didn't think it was appropriate to bring you with me for something so personal." He hesitated for a moment before speaking again. "But you can come with me if you really want to."

Fergus didn't immediately answer. He seemed to be pondering the idea, rubbing his fingers against his chin thoughtfully. "On second thought," said Fergus. He waved his bony hand dismissively. "I think I'll pass this time. I've got some unfinished milk I need to tend to."

***

The last lesson of the night was Physical Monster Education (PME), taught by a giant obese ogre by the name of Mr. Maad Wolfer. Fergus was excused from the class since he suffered from a peculiar variation of brittle bones and instead spent the entire lesson inside doing written tasks, leaving Terry to himself.

"All right, boys, let's start by doing some warm-up exercises," said Wolfer, stuffing a couple of hotdogs down his throat and licking his fat, stubby fingers, followed by a couple of snorts as he muttered how good the dogs were. "Right, I want you to start with five-hundred and fifty star jumps, followed by seven-hundred and seventy-five lunges, and then one-thousand and one-hundred squats."

Many of the students groaned in response. Sure, most of them had better stamina than the average human being, but even monsters had their limits, and this was pushing it. Wolfer's request was flat out unreasonable for them. It was natural for there to be complaints, but Wolfer would have none of it.

"Silence! You'll do what I tell you," he said, picking his nose and flicking a large green booger into the air. "Now start jumping or I'll give you all detention for the whole week. And that would be five nights in a row of non-stop squats with Miss Robyn Robin hovering over your heads."

Knowing that their freedom, and their lives, were at risk, they all started star jumping immediately. It didn't take long for Terry to start panting. He knew he wasn't the fittest person around, but after only two hundred and twenty star jumps, he already felt like keeling over. He looked to an Egyptian mummy who kept tripping on his own loose bandages. Next to him was the hair plucking werewolf from the plane doing lunges while flexing his biceps in an attempt to show off. For those that had somehow finished, Wolfer made them run laps for the rest of the lesson. Many students began collapsing halfway through their workout. Kurt, the smug vampire from the plane, managed to escape by asking to go to the toilet and never returning. Terry considered doing the same, but by then it was too late, Wolfer had noticed the class becoming empty and began rejecting bathroom requests.

By the time the lesson ended, Terry's inhaler was empty from his constant gasps for breath. He rummaged through his bag in the changing room for his spare but was unable to find it. Strange, he could have sworn he'd packed it. Maybe he'd dropped it somewhere? No matter, he had more in his dorm.

***

Once he'd composed himself after the strenuous workout, he headed for Winter's office, knocked on the door, and waited patiently. There was no answer. He knocked again. Still no response. He tried turning the handle, but the door was locked. Where could Winter be? Terry wondered.

"Ahem! May I help you?" said a familiar voice.

Terry spun round and immediately turned pale. It was Tompkins, the deputy headmaster.

"Well, Terry?" said the minotaur, the horns on his bullish head glinting in the light.

"I was, um, hoping to speak to Mr. Winter," said Terry, still trying to get used to seeing a bull's head on a human body. "I had a question for him regarding our last lesson."

"I see. I admire your eagerness, Terry Silverman. Unfortunately, Mr. Winter has left Grimerth for the night. Urgent business, he said. He should be back tomorrow though. You'll have to catch him then, I'm afraid," Tompkins continued, placing a hand on Terry's shoulder and smiling before walking off.

Terry wandered back down the staircase and signed himself out at the reception desk, making his way towards the exit. He then opened the castle doors and marched down the long stone steps. Halfway down, he noticed Fergus in the distance heading into the forest, which surrounded most of the castle. He tried calling out to him, but he didn't seem to hear. Now what was that skeleton up to? Curious to find out, he dashed down the remaining steps as quickly as possible, but by the time he got to the bottom, he'd lost sight of him. "Fergussss, Fergusss," he yelled, but there was no response.

Then he heard a high-pitched scream from afar.

"Fergus!" Terry yelled again. "Fergus?"

Another scream followed and then a muffled cry for help.

Feeling anxious, Terry rushed into the forest, shouting for his friend, but all he could hear was his own noisy heartbeat and the crunch of footsteps as he stepped on broken twigs. He continued running through the trees and foliage until he reached a small clearing. He tried to gulp some air, his legs ached, and there was a sharp stabbing pain below his ribs. He bent over, pressed his hand against the pain and tried easing the stitch with deep breaths. All the exercise he'd done earlier had affected his stamina. After a while, his breathing finally slowed, returning to normal. He stood up straight, taking a moment to assess his situation before continuing. Only now did it dawn upon him that he was alone inside a forest surrounded by looming black trees against what he could now see was a dark purple sky. It was quiet. Too quiet.

"Hello?" he shouted again. "Fergus, are you there? Are you okay?"

There was no sound. Nothing. Not even the noise of a cricket chirping. There was only the wind that appeared to howl in a creepy way.

He froze. It was only for an instant, but he could have sworn he'd seen something. Was it the Demon Wolf? No, it couldn't be. Could it? At that moment, cold bones jangled against his shoulder, making him jump and spin round—it was Fergus.

"Don't do that!" Terry snapped, placing a hand on his chest and breathing a sigh of relief.

"My goodness! Did I scare you?" said Fergus, clearly quite pleased with himself.

Terry shot a glare at him. "Hardly," he said with a huff. "What are you doing here, anyway?" Terry peered over Fergus's shoulder to see if anyone or anything else was behind him.

"I followed you into the forest," said Fergus.

Terry paused. "What are you talking about? I followed *you* into the forest."

Faint eerie laughter echoed from the trees opposite. Terry and Fergus turned their heads simultaneously in the direction of the sound.

"What was that?" said Terry.

"No idea. Want to have a look?"

Terry nodded in agreement. Having Fergus with him provided him with reassurance. They cautiously advanced forward across the clearing.

"What if we bump into the Demon Wolf?" said Fergus.

"Don't joke like that," said Terry.

As if in response to his fears, a shadowy figure burst out from the trees and attacked Fergus, instantly breaking him apart as Terry looked on horrified. The skeleton now laid on the ground—a collapsed pile of disjointed bones.

Before he could register what had happened, a powerful blow knocked Terry to the ground. And a heavy foot smacked into his stomach, making him scream out in pain. Then something tugged at his body, and the next thing Terry knew, he was being held up by an invisible force in the air, unable to move.

"Well, well, well, I can't believe it worked." Standing before Terry was Kurt, and next to him, with his hands held out into the air, was a knee-high grotesque elf with a bony face, grey scaly skin, and lizard-like yellow eyes. "Don't mind Yohan, despite his appearance, he's actually quite feeble. His magic is pretty handy though, managed to fool you," said Kurt with a triumphant smile plastered across his face, his fangs resting on his lower lip.

Terry grunted, trying to break free, but the invisible force binding him was too powerful.

"Hold him steady, Yohan," said Kurt.

Yohan nodded in response and then Kurt pulled his arm back, curling all five fingers into a fist, leaving Terry only a moment to brace himself before he slammed a punch into his gut.

Instantly, Terry stopped squirming and instead groaned in pain.

"You make me sick, you know that?" said Kurt. "You think you can embarrass me on the plane in front of a beautiful vamp like Emmy and get away with it?" Kurt grabbed Terry by his hair and held his head up so he could pummel him with several successive blows, making him spit blood.

Terry's vision blurred. He tried focusing, but the blows to his head made it difficult.

"Look what I have here," said Kurt, pulling out something from his trouser pocket. "Your spare inhaler." He dangled it before Terry. "I see you're too shocked for words. While you were busy running laps for that fat oaf Wolfer, I went into the locker room and searched your bag." Kurt's eyes glistened with satisfaction at Terry's shocked expression. "You know, I've never heard of a vampire in need of an inhaler. I wonder what happens to you if you didn't have it." He crushed the inhaler in his hand and then threw the pieces onto the ground.

Silvery rays of pale moonlight shone through as the clouds began to clear and the full moon peeked into view. Terry's heart began beating rapidly. He gritted his teeth. Something ... something was happening to him. His veins throbbed, and his fists clenched as he bared his fangs and snarled. Power. He could feel power building inside him like a ball of fire. Pain. He felt intense pain as his thin body bulked up to ten times the size and his bone structure changed, snapping into a new wider alignment as thick dark hair sprouted all over his body. And Pity. He felt pity for the monster who yearned to be free, and the boy—the boy who had to die for the monster to be born.

6

Little Blue Witch

"He's transformed into a monster! He's going to break free!" cried Yohan.

"Do something!" Kurt demanded, backing away slowly.

"It's too much for me to hold him." Yohan continued with his arms reaching out into the air in a futile attempt to keep the beast at bay with his binding spell.

"Didn't you say you were good at magic?"

"Yeah, well, I say a lot of things," said Yohan. "But between you and me, I've only read *The Beginner's Guide to Magic* and even that I skimmed."

Covered in thick black fur, the beast towered over Kurt and Yohan, and its demonic yellow eyes sent a shudder down the spine. The creature gave a maddening, ear-piercing roar. It broke free from Yohan's spell and leapt forward, pinning the vampire boy, Kurt, to the ground. It stared into the vampire's soul. Hot, stinky saliva from the beast's mouth trickled down Kurt's cheeks.

"Yuck!" he cried. He struggled to move but couldn't fight against the beast's weight. "Yohan help me!" Kurt yelled, but the elf had long since run away.

There was a sense of hopelessness and dread in Kurt's eyes, as if he were wondering whether he was actually going to die. Then as though he had found new strength inside him, he bit into the beast's hairy hand, using as much force as he could to pierce into the skin and draw blood. The beast howled in pain and anger, and in that moment, Kurt used as much force as he could muster to push the creature off him.

The sound of his claws clacking sent a chill down the spine. The beast snarled angrily at the vampire. He bared his fangs and howled at the full moon. A deafening sound that made Kurt cover his ears, and he got up and tried running away, but the beast charged towards him. Fast and agile, the creature sprang into the air, but then from nowhere, a great force pushed the beast backwards. In the path before the beast was a witch with blue eyes and dark blue hair. A smile sketched her face. The beast punched the ground below, breaking into it to stop the momentum. It was unscathed despite the impact, and let out a thunderous howl as it sprang towards its new prey, ignoring the vampire who'd scampered away.

Almira bit onto her fingerless glove and pulled it off while simultaneously unclipping the dagger from her utility belt with her right hand.

The beast drew closer, claws within striking distance.

Almira moved out of the way and glided backwards in a fluid motion to distance herself from the beast. She then used the dagger to cut her own palm. A magic circle with peculiar symbols and characters in an unknown language engraved itself onto the back of her hand and then lit up, emitting a neon blue glow. Below her, another magic circle materialised and expanded several sizes. She let the blood from her palm drip onto the circle, changing the circle's colour from blue to red and lighting up the surrounding area.

The beast approached cautiously, confused by the change in surroundings.

"Just a little closer." Almira motioned the beast towards her, challenging him. "Come on, don't tell me the big bad wolf is scared of a little girl," she said with a grin.

The beast growled and charged forward only to find itself trapped within the spellbinding circle and unable to break out. It roared in frustration and banged against the barrier repeatedly.

Almira sneered in satisfaction as she watched the beast struggle and closed the cut in her palm with a quick spell and a wave of her hand. "Aww, what's the matter? Upset you can't get me?" she said tauntingly.

The beast continued pounding against the barrier. *BANG! BANG! BANG!* Small cracks appeared in the barrier before shattering entirely.

Almira's body reacted on instinct and darted sideways but was unable to fully escape the beast's claws. She winced in pain and stared down at her bloodied clothes. "You cut me!" Almira cried. She placed her palm over the wound and sealed it with a spell while trying to distance herself from the beast, but he quickly closed the gap and struck her down. She jumped up instantly using both her legs to kick him, grinning at him like a mad child. Instead of fear or concern for her safety, it was as though she felt some kind of exhilaration from fighting this creature. Almost as if she enjoyed the challenge.

Cold air filled the night. The beast understood that this girl was dangerous. It closed in on her cautiously, suspicious another trap was brewing.

Almira removed her other glove, revealing another magic circle. She connected the engraved circles together by overlapping both her fists in a cross, creating a glowing green light. Instantly a sword materialised into her outstretched hand. The spellcaster gripped it tightly and charged forward.

The beast bellowed in response and accepted her challenge, bounding forward.

Almira twisted and turned, avoiding several lethal blows. The beast's claws came down on her, slicing into her neck. Blood trickled down her body, but she quickly closed the wound and swung her sword, piercing through the creature's chest. It groaned in pain before letting out a deafening roar. She pushed against him and jumped backwards into the air to create distance once more, her cloak fluttering in the wind. Landing dexterously, she punched the air with full force, creating a shockwave that sent the beast flying into the trees, knocking down other trees behind it in succession, like a game of dominos.

The creature's body was heavy. He tried moving but couldn't muster the strength to do so. Warm blood leaked onto the ground. He slowly stumbled forward and then fell to the ground, the dark hair on his skin vanishing, his wide bone structure reverting to high cheekbones, his bulky physique shrinking back into the slender vampire boy.

7

An Unexpected Visit

Terry watched the crackle of the flames in the fireplace as he curled up into his blanket and let the warmth spread throughout his body. This was nice. If only he could lay here forever. He'd only just woken up but still felt overwhelmingly tired. The fire only aided his desire for sleep.

"Comfortable?" said a voice.

Terry lazily lifted his head from the sofa to see who'd spoken. Across the room was Almira, the spellcaster with blue eyes and dark blue hair. She was sitting cross-legged in mid-air, upside down, and drinking a very extravagant looking blueberry milkshake in a fancy glass with a little umbrella and curly straw. Cute. On her cheeks were several cuts. Peculiar, Terry thought. He'd no recollection of seeing them on her before. Yet the cuts didn't look new, they appeared as though they'd been there for quite some time.

"You're upside-down," he said, peering at her.

She stopped sipping. "Nothing gets past you, does it?" Then she started slurping. Noisily. Maybe it was just Terry's imagination, but it felt as if she was looking down on him. Or maybe that was the way she was with everyone she met. Either way it was kind of annoying.

"How are you doing that?" he asked.

"Magic," she said disdainfully.

Terry rolled his eyes. "What happened to your face?"

"I got in a fight with a vampire and a werewolf. I won!"

He sat up and gaped at her in disbelief. "*You* defeated a vampire and a werewolf?"

"Yup, both at the same time. All by myself," she boasted.

Surely, she had to be lying. There was no way she could do that ... could she?

"Don't try and think too hard about it," she said. "Might hurt that little brain of yours."

"Excuse me?" said Terry, astonished by her lack of manners.

She stopped sipping her milkshake again and rotated upright, dropping herself to the ground. The milkshake remained in position, floating on its own in the air. She then levitated about half an inch above ground and drifted towards Terry, inadvertently exposing several lacerations across her right arm.

Yikes, they looked painful. She was now face-to-face with him, and he was taken aback. *So close!* What was it with the people here and their lack of awareness of personal space? Her ice-blue eyes gazed into his own and he found himself spellbound, at a loss for words.

"It's unwise to stare at a girl for so long," she said. "Especially when she's a witch."

He stuttered at first before finding some words. "Sorry," he said. Why was he apologising? She was the one who came close to him. His attention turned to her neck. Partially hidden behind her choker, he could see claw marks carved into her skin. He noticed her arms were covered by her cloak again, hiding the scars he'd seen earlier. How many did she have? Was it a result of fighting the vampire and werewolf?

"How'd you do it?" he asked. "How'd you beat a vampire and a werewolf at the same time?"

"Because I'm awesome," she said, a smug smile on her face. She then turned around and returned to her upside-down position, resuming slurping on her milkshake.

"That's it?" said Terry, raising an eyebrow. "You're not going to expand?"

"Expand? What am I? A balloon?"

"Huh?" said Terry, puzzled.

Almira shook her head. "Never mind."

"Where are we anyway?" Terry scanned the room. He noticed the curtains had been drawn so he couldn't see outside.

"You like it?" said Almira. "I made this place myself. It's a cottage in the forest."

"You made it?" questioned Terry, unable to believe her words.

"Yup."

"How?"

"Magic!"

"And how does that work?"

Almira shrugged. "How am I to know? It's magic, it's not supposed to make sense."

"But you're a spellcaster, shouldn't you know?"

"What is this? Twenty questions? Stop interrogating me!" she exclaimed, throwing her arms out in exasperation.

"I'm just confused," said Terry, rubbing his temple. "I don't get why I'm here, and I don't understand why you'd want to drink a milkshake upside-down. It just doesn't make sense."

"I like to pretend I'm a bat."

Terry frowned. Okay, he thought. Now he was even more confused.

"I just feel more comfortable that way, you know?"

"Not really."

She turned back the right way and dropped to the ground. "So, you seriously don't remember anything?"

"What am I supposed to remember?" Terry asked.

She levitated towards him like a ghost, her unnatural gaze aiding the ghoulish impression. Almira placed a hand on Terry's head. "Close your eyes," she instructed.

"What are you going to do?" he asked.

"Just trust me."

Terry resigned and listened. He saw nothing but darkness, but after a while, his vision began to adjust, and he found himself in a forest in the dead of night, the full moon in plain view. He heard a growl that resonated with primal savagery. Alarmed, he turned his head and immediately felt the blood drain from his face. Standing before him was a beast that put every nerve in his body on edge. It roared a terrifying bloodthirsty cry that pierced his ears.

Terry opened his eyes and gasped for air.

Almira had already pulled away and was now silently levitating before him.

For a while he said nothing, simply giving himself time to absorb the memory. What on earth had happened to him? Then a more pressing thought occurred. "Wait, what happened to Fergus?" he asked.

"Who's Fergus?" said Almira, looking bewildered.

"The skeleton that was with me."

"Oh *him*," said Almira, holding out a palm and tapping it with the bottom of her fist. She then put her hands on her hips and said proudly, "Don't worry. I buried him."

"Why would you do that?" cried Terry, his eyes bulging out from his sockets.

"I thought he was a victim of yours," said Almira defensively.

"Victim?"

"Yeah, you know, I thought you totally killed him."

"Why would I kill him?"

"Hello?" said Almira, throwing up her arms. "Blood thirsty animal? Anyway, he's been buried for three days now."

"Three days!"

"Yeah, that's how long you've been out for. Are you telling me that bag of bones was alive?"

"Well not anymore! You killed him!"

Terry fell back on the sofa, slapping his palm against his forehead. The temperature in his body dropping to a cold chill. He needed some tomato juice.

Almira burst out laughing. "Relax, he's alive."

"You were lying? That's so not funny, you know."

"I was only partially lying. I tried burying him, but almost immediately, he dug himself back out and started putting himself back together again. Gave me quite a shock."

"Where is he now?"

"Back in his dorm. Like I said before, you've been out for a while."

"And during that time," said a voice Terry instantly recognised, "Almira has been kind enough to keep an eye on you."

Terry shot up from the sofa. There, by the doorway, stood a large man in his forties with curled hair. He wore a tweed suit, matching flap cap, and a weary smile. This gentleman was Terry's uncle, Brian Silverman.

"Uncle Brian?" said Terry curiously.

"Good to see you too, young man," said Silverman.

"What are you doing here?"

Silverman's expression turned grim. Behind him appeared the minotaur, Basil Tompkins. "Please take a seat, my boy," said Silverman, gesturing Terry back towards the pair of single sofas near the fireplace. Terry sat back down and anxiously watched his uncle sit down on the sofa opposite. Tompkins remained standing behind him.

Terry waited for his uncle to speak, but Silverman remained silent as if waiting for Terry to speak first.

"Uncle Brian," said Terry, darting a quick glance at Almira before turning back to his uncle. "What exactly am I?"

Silverman sighed. "Forgive me, my boy," he began. "I thought it would be better to keep this from you, but it seems that may no longer be the best option." Tompkins placed a firm hand on Silverman's shoulder for comfort. "You are a were-vamp," said Silverman. "A hybrid. Your father was a werewolf, not a vampire as I'd initially led you to believe."

Terry stared at the floor, taking a moment to process the information. He found it odd that his uncle would hide something like this from him. Clearly there was more to the story, and Terry was eager to know, but there was something more pressing bugging him. "I thought 'were' means man."

Silverman arched an eyebrow.

"You said were-vamp. Wouldn't that just mean I'm a human that transforms into a vampire?" Terry explained. "That doesn't make much sense in my case, does it? Shouldn't it be called a vamp-wolf or wolf-vamp or something along those lines?"

"He's taking this better than I thought," said Almira. She had returned to her upside-down position and resumed drinking her blueberry milkshake. "And technically, he's right. Although, I wonder why he never considered his father was a werewolf when his uncle is one."

She was right, thought Terry. It was so obvious. Now he felt silly for never considering it before.

Silverman briefly shot a glance at her. "Don't be so pedantic," he said before turning back to Terry. "Worrying about such small details is a waste of time. Now listen, you mustn't tell anyone what you are. Hybrids are generally frowned upon. While it may be true that we're not at war anymore, there is still some very real hostility between werewolves and vampires. If you were to be found out, there would undoubtedly be people who'd want you dead. You must keep your identity a secret, do you understand?"

Terry nodded. There were a thousand questions he wanted to ask, but he knew what his uncle was like. He had to play his cards carefully, make the right moves. It would probably be best to take a backward route.

"What triggered my transformation? Was it the full moon?" said Terry.

"No. Not at all. The full moon has no real bearing on your transformations. It was something more primal. A desire. A need to survive. Your life was in danger for the first time and your primal instinct to survive kicked in, allowing the beast to take control." Silverman then turned to Almira with a disappointed look. "As a precaution against this happening, Almira here had been tasked with keeping watch over you, but it seems she slipped up a little."

"Hey, I can't watch him twenty-four seven," said Almira, giving an upside-down shrug. "I've got my own things to do. Besides, I had Lola keep an eye on him for me, and I got there as soon as I could once I got the alert from her."

Terry's initial thought was who on earth was Lola? He hadn't noticed anyone following him around at all. How long had this Lola been watching him? Where were they now? Had Terry met them before? Was it someone in his class? Then something else came to Terry's mind. "This might be unrelated," he began, "but do you know who Mihai Winter is?"

Silverman's eyes widened.

A curious reaction; clearly, he was familiar with the name.

"How—how do you know that name?" he asked.

"He's their teacher for History of Man and Monster," answered Tompkins.

"He's a strange one," said Terry. "When he saw me, he started acting weird. He told me he knew my mother. He seemed awfully interested in you, uncle. It's why I wondered if you might know him. Judging by your reaction, I guess, I'm right?"

Silverman looked at Terry questionably. He leaned forward in his seat and clasped his hands together under his chin. "What else has he told you?"

"Not a lot. There was some mention of some war, but he didn't have much time to explain before the class ended. I wanted to meet him again to ask some questions, but he'd already left the school grounds before I could. Who is he anyway?"

Silverman leaned back and stroked his moustache. "I must say, this is quite an interesting development. Quite an interesting development, indeed." He seemed to be lost in thought, staring blankly into space. "I wonder, Tompkins, why you never told me of this?"

"I confess I wasn't aware you knew him," said Tompkins.

"Only by reputation," said Silverman. "You see, he's the boy's grandfather."

"My grandfather?" said Terry, standing up. "Why am I only hearing of him now?"

"I wasn't aware of his whereabouts, but I'm sure we can get acquainted at a more appropriate time. There is a more pressing matter that I must discuss with you, my boy."

"What's that?" asked Terry.

Silverman glanced at Almira and then Tompkins with whom he exchanged nods. "I have asked Almira here to train you."

"Train me? Why?"

"To help you control the other side of yourself," explained Silverman. "I believe I need not explain further. You do remember what happened, do you not?"

Terry fell silent.

"She may only be a year your senior, but Almira has a lifetime of experience. You see, there is a way to control the transformations and make them happen at will. She can teach you how. I ask you to show her the same respect you would show myself or any elder."

Almira had a stupid grin plastered across her face. "Oh, won't this be fun?" she said gleefully. "Maybe I should have you address me as Master?"

Terry turned to Silverman with a worried expression. "You're serious about this?"

Silverman looked at him grimly. "Very serious. Now I have some other business that I must attend to, but I shall be back soon to see how you're doing. Until then, work hard and take care, my boy. Stay strong."

He then addressed Almira. "I leave him in your capable hands."

8

Birth of the Wolfpire

Fergus was ecstatic when Terry returned from his three-day absence to their dorm room. The moment he saw him, he immediately rushed up to Terry and hugged him tightly. "You're okay!" cried the skeleton, pulling back and pretending to wipe a tear from his empty eye socket. "I still can't believe you're a wolfpire."

"A what?" said Terry, doing a double take.

"A wolfpire. You know, a werewolf and vampire combo. We have to tell everyone."

"No, we don't. Also, the correct term for it is were-vamp."

"But that doesn't make any sense! That just means man vampire, doesn't it? Wait! Hell's bells and buckets of blood! Don't tell me you're a human too? Gosh, wow. You know, I used to be human. Then I died. Or did I? Can't really remember. Dark days, you know. Blasted Grim Reaper wanting a successor. I mean, did he *really* have to kill me first before deciding I'm not worthy? Oh well, can't wait to tell everyone about you being a wolfpire."

"Okay, I feel like that's a can of worms I shouldn't open. Also, why do you need to tell anyone anything?" asked Terry, going over to the corner of the room to open the mini fridge and grabbing a carton of tomato juice from inside.

"Well, it's such big news that it would be a shame to keep it hidden."

Terry shook his head and made Fergus sit down on one of the wooden chairs near the desk by the bunk bed. "Look mate," he began, taking a seat himself and removing the straw attached to the tomato juice carton. "If you go around telling others that I'm a were-vamp—"

"Wolfpire," said Fergus, interrupting him to correct his terminology.

Terry pierced the carton with the straw. "Right. If you go telling others that I'm a wolfpire, then it's going to cause problems." He sipped his drink and then sighed in relief.

"I don't see a problem with being a famous wolfpire," said Fergus. "You could be on the covers of magazines. Then I'd become famous by association, and girls will finally start taking an interest in me. It's hard to get dates being this bony, you know. Not much to offer really."

Finally, Terry realised Fergus's true intentions. And so began a rather long conversation that carried over past registration and into their third class of the night, which was Study of the Seven Realms taught by Miss Robyn Robin, the floating white sheet of a ghost with black oval eyeholes.

"I hope you will all recall from our last lesson," she began in her usual monotone voice, "that there are seven realms, dimensions ... seven known alternate planes of existence—all sharing the same planet. Three of these are uninhabitable, deserted lands that are of no use to anyone. Then we have one which belongs to the humans, one that is home of the djinn, and one that is a bit of a mystery to us. We know it exists. There are witness statements confirming glimpses into this strange, enigmatic world, and we have evidence of its existence, but we still do not know who or what exactly inhabits this land. And then finally we have this realm, our world, the home of monsters like you and I."

Most teachers would write on the board during class to help provide the students with some visual aid, but since Robyn Robin was a ghost, she was unable to touch or pick anything up. All she could do was hover around aimlessly. She did, however, have the power to disrespect doors and pass right through them. She also apparently had the power to kill students by just showing them what she looked like underneath her sheet. Terry still wasn't sure if he believed that would actually happen if anyone was actually foolish enough to peek, but with everything else he had seen so far in this world, he had no desire to find out.

"Now, for tonight's class, we will cover a little bit about the relationships and differences between each realm. We'll begin with the human and the monster world. In the old days, when our understanding of the seven realms and the passageways to them was more limited, many monsters would often find themselves accidentally slipping through portals to the human world. Unfortunately, most human beings are … irrational. Similar to us in many ways actually, but their fear of anything strange and unnatural led to many of our kind being hunted down and killed. Even humans spellcasters were not safe from their non-spellcaster counterparts."

Robin slowly hovered between the middle of the classroom, passing each desk as she spoke, ready to threaten any student who dared misbehave.

Fergus, however, was unconcerned. He was instead busy scribbling something down in his exercise book. Now, to the untrained eye, it might have appeared that the skeleton was just busy taking notes about what Robin was saying, but Terry knew better. Terry knew that Fergus was actually just continuing their conversation from earlier, only now in note form.

"Though we do utilise some of their better ideas, our own interactions with humans are very limited today," said Robin, who was at the other end of the classroom. "Our old portals, with the exception of one, have been sealed to prevent any further misplacements and incidents. True enough, UGOM still keeps contact with some of the human leaders and figureheads, but to most humans, we are nothing more than myths and legends. Our only relationship with them is to co-ordinate and keep us both apart. It is also to bring any monster unfortunate enough to be found in the human world to ours where they will not be hunted and killed. Though why some monsters are still born in the human world to this day remains a bit of question mark for us."

Emmy, the pretty vampire girl from the plane, lifted her hand to ask some questions about the similarities that both worlds shared, which kept Robin's attention away from Fergus.

The skeleton tore out the page he was scribbling on as quietly as he could. He then folded it in half with his bony hands, checked his surroundings, and passed it to Terry as nonchalantly as possible.

Terry unfolded the paper and read the note.

> You're stealing our opportunity to be famous
> here!

Terry shook his head with a sigh and jotted down his response.

> And you're stealing my opportunity for a
> normal life!

He casually passed the note back to Fergus who retorted with the following:

> You left normal behind when you stepped into
> this world. I'm offering you a chance to be
> famous here.
> You'll be a star.

And so they continued like this, passing notes back and forth while trying to avoid Robin's attention.

> I don't want to be a star.

> Why not?

> I just don't. My uncle said it would be bad.

> How so?

> According to him, hybrids are hated. I don't
> want to be hated.

What are you planning to compensate me with for the loss I'm willing to suffer?

Terry stared at Fergus's message with a blank expression. He blinked twice. What exactly was this nutter expecting to be compensated with? It's not like Terry had anything valuable to offer him. He twirled his pencil around his thumb while trying to think about the things which Fergus liked that Terry could offer.

Let's see, he thought. The first item that came to mind was trading cards, but Terry didn't have any, nor did he have any idea where to buy them. Also, Fergus had mentioned before that buying cards had drained him of his money, and Terry's uncle hadn't given him much money to begin with, so buying expensive trading cards was off the table.

Hmm. There had to be something else. Something cheap. Come on, Terry. Think. Oh, of course! Why hadn't he thought of it in the first place? He could offer the skeleton some milk! Surely that would shut Fergus up about revealing Terry's secret. He wrote down his offer and passed it along, but as he did, he felt his hand pass through something cold. His eyes widened, noticing his hand had disappeared into a white sheet hovering beside him, and the realisation dawned on him that he had just collided with Robyn Robin.

9

Substitute

Oh God no, he thought. Terry was doomed, his secret would be out. It was all over. The teacher would know, and she'd probably reveal it to everyone. What were the others going to think? What was his uncle going to think? It had just been one night, and already Terry had failed to maintain his secret. Once everyone knew he was some weird hybrid, he'd be hated for sure. His life would be in constant danger. He had to think of a way to salvage the situation. He waited for a moment before looking up, and when he did, he saw that the ghost wasn't looking at him at all. Instead, her attention was on Fergus who had raised his hand to ask a question.

"Yes, Mr. Gravestone?" said Robyn Robin.

Terry used the opportunity to his advantage and retracted his hand, hiding the note under his textbook. He sighed in relief, wiping the sweat from his brow with the back of his hand. That was a close call, far too close. He wasn't going to risk passing any more notes in class. It was much too risky. He had to be more careful.

Once lunch time rolled around, Terry managed to strike a deal with Fergus by offering to buy him three cartons of milk to go with his meal and three more the next night. Fergus, however, wanted something more and pointed to Terry's death by chocolate pudding dessert to seal the deal. Terry was reluctant at first but acquiesced. If it would keep that blabbermouth shut, then it was worth it. The negotiations were a success as far as he was concerned. Now at least his secret would be safe—he hoped.

There was, of course, one other matter that was on Terry's mind. Mihai Winter, or as Terry had learnt, his grandfather! Like, seriously? Why wasn't he told about this before? Oh, well, at least he now had another chance to learn about his folks from his newfound family member— he had long given up the idea of his uncle telling him anything. He couldn't quite explain it, but there was a warm and fuzzy feeling bubbling inside him. After all this time, there was finally someone else for him to turn to other than his uncle. He couldn't wait to see his grandfather. Fortunately for Terry, the last class of the night would be with Winter himself. It was a perfect opportunity to talk without him having to rush off to the next class.

All the students had arrived that night and settled down at their desks in the classroom, yet it was ten minutes into the lesson and Winter was still nowhere in sight. Suddenly, the door opened, and in strode Basil Tompkins. All the students fell silent in his presence as he made his way to the front and stood at Winter's empty desk.

"Good night. I have some rather unfortunate news, students. It seems Mr. Winter has taken an unforeseen leave of absence. In his stead, a new teacher will take over his class for the time being." Tompkins turned to the door and shouted, "That's your cue, sir."

Terry's jaw dropped wide open.

In walked his uncle, Brian Silverman, looking a little ruffled and out of place. "Apologies for the delays, everyone. I will be your substitute teacher until Mr. Winter returns."

Immediately, Terry raised his hand.

"Yes, Terry?" said Tompkins clasping his hands together as he snorted through his snout.

87

"Sorry, but what's happened to Mr. Winter? How long has he gone for?"

"Mr. Winter's leave is due to personal circumstances, of which I am not at liberty to discuss. I am told, however, that he is to hopefully return sometime after the Halloween festival. Now, if you don't mind, Mr. Silverman needs to start class."

Terry felt his heart sink. He was an orphan and always felt like an outsider compared to others who had proper parents and siblings. This was an opportunity to know about family, connect with a long lost grandparent and finally feel wanted. Was he cursed, never knowing what it was to truly feel loved? Why did life have to keep pulling the rug from under him?

***

By the end of the week, it was time for Terry's first training session with Almira. They had snuck away into the forest after class and were heading to her cottage. Of course, Fergus wanted to join them, but the skeleton suspected he'd contracted a bad case of diarrhoea from having too much milk and was too busy sitting on the toilet to join them. Terry shook his head just thinking about it. It seemed to Terry that the skeleton knew he was a skeleton, but for whatever reason, Fergus liked to pretend he had organs just like everyone else. Whatever, thought Terry, that wasn't really his concern right now.

Terry was still a little apprehensive about having Almira teach him. As far as he could tell, she wasn't some wise old sage with years of experience under her belt, unless she was disguising herself as a stuck up, patronising, milkshake-drinking irritant, in which case, she was doing a darn good job. Still, she did manage to incapacitate Terry when he'd lost control and transformed into a hairy werewolf, but what was she going to teach him that his uncle couldn't? Was she going to use magic to dispel his demons? Or maybe she was going to have him drink some special herb to exorcise the beast within? Speaking of his uncle …

"It's a little weird," said Terry.

"What's weird?" asked Almira as they continued their walk amongst the trees in the forest.

"After years of believing I'm a daywalker, I've suddenly found out I'm actually some sort of rare vampire-werewolf hybrid."

"Right, a were-vamp."

"About that name, I'm starting to think wolfpire sounds better."

"Hmm, *the worst wolf*. Cute. Did you think of that yourself?"

"Fergus came up with it, but it's growing on me the more I say it," Terry confessed. "Anyway, straight after I learn that I have a grandfather I never knew about, he's now taken a leave of absence before I can ask him anything, and all of a sudden, my new substitute teacher is my uncle."

Terry waited briefly to see if Almira would say anything before continuing, but she didn't.

"I was looking forward to properly introducing myself and getting to know him. Actually, I was hoping he might even tell me about my parents since my uncle never does. It would be nice to finally know what they were really like and what else I might have inherited from them. I mean, what if I have some health issues that only affect wolfpires? How am I going to know? Now I have to wait until my grandfather returns."

"I'm sure you'll get answers soon," replied Almira as she looked into the distance, seemingly uninterested.

"I just hope that whatever caused him to take such abrupt leave wasn't too serious. I've tried asking some of the teachers, but no one gave me anything more to go on. I just pray he returns," he whispered.

Almira turned to look at him. "What's the matter … you think he won't return?"

"I don't know. I hope he does, but I just can't shake this sinking feeling inside me."

"Chin up, I'm sure he's fine. Besides, I need you to be positive for your training."

Terry swept his fringe out of his eyes with his hand. "I still can't believe I'm supposed to train under you."

"What's that supposed to mean?" Almira replied, her eyes flashing with a mixture of anger and amusement.

"Nothing, it just feels strange. I don't know why. Maybe it's 'cause we're almost the same age, so you don't really feel like a teacher to me."

She smirked. "I'll take that as a compliment. Anyway, there's something I need to do before we begin," she continued as they reached her cottage. She walked straight to the front door, opened it, and popped inside.

Terry followed her in and found Almira crouched down on the floor in the living room, petting a small cockatiel. The bird chirped happily and snuggled against Almira's fingers. Terry wondered if it might be a familiar, a supernatural pet that assisted spellcasters in witchcraft. Most witches he had read about used cats, but birds were not unheard of, though they would normally be owls, not cockatiels.

"I missed you too, Lola," said Almira.

"Lola?" said Terry, peering over Almira to get a better look at the bird. "Wait, is this the same Lola that's been following me?"

91

"That's right."

"Huh," said Terry, straightening up. "Why'd you name her Lola?"

Almira continued to pet the bird. "I named her after my best friend."

"What happened? Did she go to a different school?" Terry asked.

"She died," said Almira.

Well, that was somewhat awkward, thought Terry. "Oh," he said, searching for the right words. "I'm so sorry to hear that."

"Don't be," said Almira. For a moment, there was complete silence. She stopped petting the bird and stood up, walking past Terry and back towards the front door. Terry followed her outside the cottage where she waved her arms around and created a small fire using magic as if it were a camping trip.

"Take a seat," she said, sitting down cross-legged on the grass in the front garden and near the fire.

Terry sat down opposite her in the same position.

"You need to learn how to harmonise with the other half of you," said Almira.

Terry arched an eyebrow. "And how would I do that?"

"By confronting the beast within," said Almira, "face-to-face. Right now, you fear that inner werewolf, but that's natural. We all fear the unknown and what we can't see. Maybe not consciously, but subconsciously. You're afraid of what the other you can do because you've never connected with that side of yourself before, but that's why you must face it head-on."

"Okay, but how?" said Terry, still confused.

"First, close your eyes," Almira instructed.

Terry rolled his eyes but did as he was told.

"Clear your mind and relax," said Almira. "Now listen." She spoke ever so softly. "Listen to the sound of my voice as it lingers in the air. Hear the flames of the fire making the wood crackle, hear the wind howling and the trees rustling. Let it all sink in. Absorb it."

Within moments, Terry slipped into a timeless space, enveloped in complete blackness. A sense of loneliness welled up within. He awoke, opened his eyes, and found himself alone in the forest. There was no cottage, no fire, no Almira, as if they'd never been there together. He looked up at the skies and saw the full moon in all its shimmering glory. The wind brushed against his cheeks. He shivered, feeling the cold air engulf him.

Then he heard it. The howling. And in the distance, the beast approached.

10

In Our Darkest Dreams

Terry ran as fast as he could. His breath came in small spurts, and his ribs began to ache, but he couldn't stop, for he knew the beast was coming. His hands clenched into fists. It was as if he believed that clenching them as they swung from side to side would make him run faster. The growling of the beast could be heard from behind, but he dared not look back. Pushing his already exhausted legs harder, he felt the burning sting that came with increased strain to the body. Slowly, the growling began to fade into the background. Curiosity tempted him to look around and check, but he forced himself to continue running, if only for a little longer.

His legs began to fail him, so he hid himself behind a tree and closed his eyes, praying it would be okay. No sound could be heard, only his own huffing and puffing. He peered from behind the tree cautiously and was relieved to see nothing was following him. Eyes closed once more, he allowed himself a moment to rest. How long had he been running for? He was struggling to breathe, his body aching all over. He removed his inhaler from his pocket and took a puff of the medicine to relax his throat. In a puddle by his feet was the reflection of a scared little boy. Was this all he amounted to? Then the reflection began to morph into another creature.

The beast grabbed Terry by the throat with a powerful hand and held him up in the air. He gasped, his head about to explode. The beast was crushing his throat. He tried fighting back but couldn't muster the strength—all he could do was wait helplessly as his vision began to blur and everything around him turned to black.

***

Terry blinked a few times and sat upright, his heart pounding heavily. He wiped the sweat from his brow with the back of his hand and welcomed the bright rays of the afternoon sun into the bedroom, seeing the beauty of the forest through the cottage window.

Just a dream, he thought. The same stupid dream.

He fell back onto the bed and laid there for a while, staring blankly at the ceiling. Normally, he'd be in his dorm, but for weekends he'd stay at the cottage under Almira's tuition. It had been a week since Almira sent him to confront the beast, and from then on, Terry had been having nightmares of the encounter over and over again. It was driving him crazy. He'd always imagined himself to be brave in the face of danger, to be seen as the hero of his own story. How wrong he was. In truth, he was just a coward. It was foolish for him to think he'd ever be anything more. He forced himself to get up, and after taking a shower, he made his way downstairs.

Almira was meditating in the living room, levitating mid-air with her legs folded and eyes closed. Very majestic, he thought, reminiscent of the ancient masters of folklore. All she was missing was a long white beard, and then the look would be complete.

"What's up, beastpire?" she said, opening her eyes and noticing the troubled look on Terry's face.

On a different day Terry might have given her an annoyed look, but not today. Today he just wasn't in the mood. "I had the same dream again," he said.

"With the beast?" asked Almira.

He nodded, his face twisting into sadness.

Almira tutted at Terry's pathetic expression. "I told you to conquer the beast, but it seems like you're the one being conquered instead."

"How exactly am I supposed to beat that creature?" Terry groaned. "He's so much stronger than me!"

"That creature is you!" she snapped. "You're one and the same. And besides, in that state, he's only physically stronger." Almira unfolded her legs and floated down, placing her feet on the floor, as if she had just slid off an invisible chair. "But when it comes to willpower," she began, bringing herself face-to-face with Terry, "that's where *you* can win."

"What am I supposed to do? Let him kill me?" said Terry.

Almira shrugged. "You need to figure out what you're doing wrong."

"Easy for you to say." Terry pulled out his inhaler. He didn't like the idea of having his identity killed off and be completely taken over by that monster.

"Wait!" said Almira.

"What?"

"Give me that," she said, swiping the inhaler from his hand.

"Hey! What are you doing? I need that!"

"No, you don't. Your uncle told me you don't actually have asthma. This is just a crutch, a placebo to help you relax and contain the beast, but you rely on it far too much. I'm getting rid of it." Almira turned around and moved towards the fireplace.

"Don't throw it in the fire!" said Terry, horrified. "It'll explode!"

Almira paused, slightly hesitant. "You don't think I know that?" she said, feigning confidence. She so didn't know that, but she was, of course, going to pretend that she did. She instead threw the inhaler into the bin near the fire. "See? I wasn't aiming for the fire. Gosh, you love to overreact to everything, don't you? Now, let's try this again, shall we?" She levitated back towards Terry and placed her hand on his forehead.

"You can send me there by touching my forehead? Why did I meditate last time then?"

"Your eyes were closed, I did the same thing back then as well," she said.

Terry stared at her with a blank expression. "Do you just enjoy annoying me?"

Almira smiled. "Try to remember what you're fighting for this time."

Before he knew it, he was back in the forest again, alone at night, hiding behind a tree. The ground was wet where it had recently rained. He stared down at the same puddle where he'd lost consciousness. Not again, he thought. No. No, this time, he was going to do this. He was going to be brave. He took a deep breath and stepped away from the tree.

"I'm here!" Terry shouted into the night. "Come get me!"

The beast howled in response.

Of course, there's a difference between being a hero and being just plain stupid. He realised that he'd opted for the latter. He turned to make a run for it, but it was too late, the beast was behind him, staring into his eyes with its cold demonic glare. It was almost twice the size of Terry and covered in thick black fur. The creature stood upright on powerful hind legs, wiping the saliva from its open jaws with the back of its giant hairy hand in an eerie fashion.

Terry stood motionless with fear. His mind told him to move, but he couldn't find the will or strength in his legs to do so. His chest tightened. It was the end of the line; he was really going to die this time. He shut his eyes and prayed that it would end quickly.

For a while, nothing happened. He peeked and saw the beast hadn't moved, still staring right at him, jaws dripping with saliva. Why hadn't it attacked? Its cold stare made Terry's skin crawl. Then he heard a growling voice, cold and rasping. But the sound wasn't coming from outside … but from inside of him.

"How many times must I destroy you?"

Terry scanned the area around him, confused, wondering who was talking through him.

"I stand before you."

Moonlight illuminated the creature and his eyes fell on the beast. Now that Terry was able to get a good look, he appeared a little less frightening than before.

"You can talk?" said Terry, eyeing him carefully.

"No, but you can hear my thoughts, for you and I are one and the same."

"If we're the same, then why do you want to kill me?" he asked.

"You are weak, Terry Silverman. Scared. I cannot have a weakling controlling me."

"I don't seek to control you," said Terry.

"Is that not why you are here? Is that not the reason the spellcaster sent you? To conquer me? But you cannot reason with a monster when you threaten its existence. Our primal instinct is to survive, and you, Terry Silverman, are a threat to my survival."

"I want us to be integrated as one being, we're stronger together than we are apart."

"But you … fear me."

"Yes, I do. But I can learn not to." Terry remembered what he was fighting for, he was here for a reason. "We fear the unknown," he said, remembering Almira's words to him. He had to face the beast, not just for himself, but for Fergus and Almira as well. To keep them safe, to protect his friends, he needed to have courage. He stepped forward cautiously, feeling his heart race with each step.

The beast snarled, staring down at him, but it didn't move. Slowly, Terry raised his hand towards the creature. "I'll make you stronger."

11

The Spellcaster for the Ages

Terry sweated profusely. He had just returned from a timeless space where he and the beast inside him had spoken to each other for the first time ever. Now he was on all fours in Almira's cottage. It was disorienting going from one location to another in the blink of an eye. He'd travelled from the freezing cold of the forest to the heat of the fireplace in the living room. He covered his mouth, feeling the need to throw up.

It seemed that Almira had been waiting in the same place the whole time, levitating silently and watching.

"Well done," she said, turning round and drifting away, "but don't celebrate yet. We've still got more ground to cover."

Without waiting to hear what more she had to say, Terry got up and ran upstairs. He threw open the bathroom door and grabbed hold of the edges of the basin for support once he was inside. A puddle of reddish vomit spurted out from his mouth and into the sink. A second one followed. He wiped his mouth with the back of his hand and opened the tap, washing away the vomit from the sink. He cupped a hand and filled it with some water which he used to gargle and spat back out in an attempt to clear the awful aftertaste.

Ugh, disgusting, he thought. Terry cupped both his hands and splashed his face with cold water. When he raised his head to see his reflection in the mirror, he was instead greeted by the beast staring back at him. He immediately jumped backwards, letting out a small yell.

He paused, noticing the beast in the mirror remaining still. He listened to the snorting of the creature's breath and in Terry's mind, he could hear the beast's thoughts speaking to him.

"You still fear."

"Can you blame me?" said Terry. "You just came out of nowhere."

The beast remained silent.

Terry moved forward carefully. "So, how does this work?" he asked. "How does our, uh, *partnership* work exactly?"

"You'll learn in time, Terry Silverman. For now, I'll permit you control, but threaten my existence again and I will destroy you."

And with that, the beast disappeared from sight as if blown away by a gust of wind, leaving Terry behind with his reflection. His hand gripped the area of his chest where his heart lay. Though he could no longer see the beast, he could still feel the creature's presence lurking deep inside him ... waiting in silence.

***

Terry stood still, as if rooted to the spot. Both he and Almira were outside again, this time at the back of the cottage where Terry noticed a tree with an old swing. It gently swayed back and forth, making small creaking sounds in the wind. He wondered for a moment who the swing was for. Perhaps it was Almira's. He hadn't really considered it before, but seeing the swing made him question why Almira was living alone in a cottage in the forest instead of the dorms like himself and everyone else. And why was she a prefect when she was only in her second year? Usually prefects would be final year students ... at least that was the case in the human world. But this wasn't the human world, so maybe the same rules didn't apply.

So many questions began to fill his mind, but he was hesitant to ask. He had learned long ago from his uncle that people didn't like others nosing about in their business. He would just have to be patient and learn by watching, reading between the lines, and finding out in a way that didn't make others defensive.

Almira was a few meters apart from Terry. She slowly circled around him, dragging her sword behind her and leaving a mark on the ground. "Now," she began, hauling up the sword and holding the pointed end towards Terry's chest. "Let's see if you're able to control the transformation at will or if you need a bit more help." Almira lowered her sword. "Try calling out the beast."

Terry nodded and then clenched his fists, grunting as hard as he could. He squinted his eyes and tried letting out a roar in an attempt to sound like the beast, but it instead came out rather pathetic, almost like a small cat trying to frighten off a big dog.

Eyes wide, Almira stared at him with an expression on her face that Terry interpreted as a mixture of shame and shock. He didn't blame her; he had never felt so embarrassed in his life. He could just feel his face burning up, and he was probably bright red.

Almira slapped her face with her palm and shook her head in dismay. "*What* on earth are you doing?" she asked.

"I was trying to, you know, channel the inner beast," said Terry defensively.

"Well, don't do it like that again or you'll embarrass us both," said Almira. "More importantly, you'll make me look incompetent as a master, and an apprentice should never make their master look bad. Honestly, I question what was going through your mind."

Terry's head dropped down. He stared at the ground, feeling sorry for himself.

Almira let out a heavy sigh and stabbed her sword into the ground. "My bad, I didn't mean to hurt your feelings." She moved a few steps closer towards Terry so that they were now within inches of each other. "It was never going to be that easy anyway. Come on, chin up."

Terry looked up and watched Almira pull one of her fingerless gloves off. On the back of her exposed hand was a strange glowing circle with various symbols. He realised he had seen this before, not as Terry Silverman, but as the beast. Back then, he hadn't paid such close attention to it, but now he could study the circle in better detail. At the centre of the magic circle were multiple stars on top of each other in different rotations, and atop the stars were dual crescent moons crossing each other like two curved swords in combat. On the inside edge going around the circle was an inscription written in what Terry believed to be the Zaynizian alphabet.

"What do those words say?" he asked.

Almira removed the other fingerless glove, the same circle present on the other hand, and read the inscription. "*User of this magic beware, this is a spell only for those who share my blood. With it comes strength and power. Power of the Spellcaster for the Ages. And for those who dare defy, a terrible price you will pay.*"

Terry's initial thought was how ominous the message sounded towards the end. Several questions popped to mind, but he reminded himself to be patient and to not ask too many. He didn't want to come across as being too nosy, so he held back until Almira spoke.

"It's okay," she said. "I can see the look on your face. You can ask this time."

Terry smiled. "Who's the Spellcaster for the Ages?"

"A forefather of mine," said Almira.

"Is that why you can use this magic? Because you share his blood?"

Almira nodded.

Terry then remembered what had happened the last time he saw the magic circles and his eyes fell on the dagger attached to Almira's belt.

"Are you going to cut your palm again like you did before?"

"I don't need to," she said. "Not for a while, at least."

A bit of a vague answer, thought Terry. "What do you mean?"

"It's just something I had to do at the time to unlock my full power. Problem is once I activate it, I have to wait at least three months before I can seal it again and get rid of these circles." She put both gloves back on again, hiding the magic circles.

"Why'd you remove the gloves if you were just going to put them back on anyway?"

Almira turned and moved towards her sword. "A momentary distraction," she said. "I figured a change of subject might help cheer you up. Seems to have done the trick, so question and answer is over now. It's time to get back to your training."

"Just one more question," said Terry.

Almira pulled the sword out from the ground. "What's that?"

"Why not just stay at full power all the time?"

"Because it's exhausting," said Almira, her back was still turned to Terry when she spoke. "My powers are constantly changing ... growing." She looked up at the night sky, the ends of her cape flickered in the wind as she did. "Once I'm an adult, my magic will mature and be easier to manage, but right now I'm still young. It's difficult to explain, but with all my abilities unlocked, I end up needing to frequently regulate my power with meditation and all that upside down floating you saw me doing before. If I don't, I'll end up falling sick, and trust me, seeing me sick is not a pretty sight."

The circle Almira had drawn on the ground earlier with her sword lit up, emitting a blue glow. A magic circle resembling the one on Almira's hands materialised in its place.

"That's enough about me for now," said Almira. She held up the sword, still looking away from Terry. "Brace yourself. I'm about to strike."

There was hardly any time between Almira's warning and the attack that followed. She moved so fast. One second she was standing within his line of sight, the next second she disappeared only to reappear again behind Terry, but by the time he had realised it was too late.

Something sharp pierced through Terry's back and out from his stomach. It took him a second to register that he had been stabbed by Almira's sword. It had cut right through him as if he were made of butter. Blood spilled out from the tear in his flesh ... so much blood.

She pulled out her sword and watched him with detached indifference as he keeled over and coughed out more blood.

For a moment, he wondered if he would die. Then the searing pain began to fade away and a familiar warmth filled him from within and he could hear the beast calling to him.

"Terry. Rise."

His wound sealed itself, and thick black hair sprouted all over his body. He dug his fingers into the dirt as his body changed in size, and within moments the vampire boy was replaced by the beast with no name.

Almira smiled and held the hilt of her sword against her body with both hands, the blade raised in the air. "Round two."

.

12

The Stories We Find

Every move she made was so precise. Each twist, each turn, and each swing of her sword was calculated and swung with precision to carefully deliver only non-lethal strikes. It was almost as though the spellcaster fighting the beast right now was a different person from the one he had faced last time. Sharper and more refined in her movements. And she was playing with him.

No matter what the beast did, he just couldn't lay a finger on the spellcaster. The beast roared in frustration; he could not allow this mockery to continue. Did this little girl really think she could be a match for his power? But little did she know that this time the beast was different from before. This time round, he was not alone. Terry Silverman was conscious inside the beast, aware of the monster's movements. All the creature's feelings and everything it saw was perfectly clear to Terry as if they were his own.

Almira glided backwards towards the edge of the circle on the ground. The beast leapt towards her, claws out, in an attempt to slash at her, but again, Almira moved so fast that it was as though she had just disappeared. When he turned to find her, she was at the opposite end of the circle. She was fast before, but never so fast that Terry couldn't even follow her.

He tried again and again, leaping with his claws out, but each time the result was the same: she just kept disappearing and reappearing. Then something clicked inside Terry's mind—she was staying within the magic circle. He had to let the beast know.

"Hey! Hey, can you hear me?" he shouted.

And the beast responded to him, not out loud but in his mind. *"I can hear you. Speak."*

Terry was surprised it had worked. Despite the situation being reversed, he found it amusing how normal this felt. Before it was the beast calling out to him while Terry had found himself afraid, but this time, he was the one speaking to the beast from within his own body. And somehow, it felt so natural, as if he were just talking to himself in his own head.

"Do you want to defeat her?" Terry asked.

"Of course."

"Then I have an idea. Do you trust me?"

There was a moment's silence before the beast finally answered him. *"I trust you, Terry Silverman."*

Almira was poised for battle, waiting for the monster to attack first, but instead of playing her game and coming to her, the beast stepped backwards, outside of the magic circle.

The spellcaster had a mild look of surprise on her face which confirmed Terry's suspicion: her instant movements must have been limited to within the circle.

Almira smirked and dashed forward with her sword held at waist level, the circle beneath her feet shattered as she moved. She was still fast, but this time Terry could see her movements, giving him time to react. He reverted back to his vampire self in almost an instant and dodged, believing it would be harder for Almira to strike him if there were less of him to hit.

She stumbled forward with a confused expression after her attack failed, and she almost lost her footing in the process.

As fast as possible, Terry transformed back to his wolfish side, hoping that the quick change had caused enough confusion to give him the advantage. He pulled back his claws into the air and brought them down in a bid to slash her.

She can heal, he told himself. There was no reason to be concerned about her safety. She certainly wasn't concerned about his when she stabbed him in the back with her sword earlier.

His claws came at her at full force, but all he hit was empty air, for she had thrown aside her sword and dropped down to deliver a low spinning sweep kick, taking Terry's leg out from under him and making him fall backwards.

Terry grunted as he landed.

Almira stood up and clapped her hands. "Not bad," she said with a smile. "Seems you can finally transform at will now."

He reverted back to his vampire form and picked himself up off the ground. "You dropped your sword," said Terry, feeling a little pleased by the compliment and the fact that he had forced her to let go of her weapon.

Almira removed both her gloves and tossed them aside to where her sword lay. "I'll let you in on a secret." Both magic circles glowed a neon blue colour; she connected the backs of her fists together in a cross and the circles changed colour from blue to green. Then she shifted her position, taking on a different fighting stance. She brought her left foot forwards, bent her knees slightly, raised her hands with clenched fists, and said, "I'm stronger without it."

And, in that moment, Terry knew that this was not going to end well for him.

✳✳✳

Broken ribs, multiple bruises, a concussion, and who knew what else Terry might have suffered had it not been for his super-fast healing. Seriously, what was that blue-haired milkshake-drinking nutter thinking? Terry may have been a wolfpire, but even he had his limits. Did that witch really have to be so rough with him?

On top of his sessions with Almira, Terry still had to deal with going to classes and doing homework. Ugh, it was exhausting to say the very least. Thankfully, tonight was a night off from his training, and he could really do with some rest after a week of being a punching bag. Classes had concluded for the night, but there was still the matter of Terry needing to finish his homework before he could go to his dorm and sleep.

Both he and Fergus were in the old library, sitting at damp wooden desks with textbooks open and exercise books to write in.

Looking around, Terry's thoughts fell back to the welcome assembly on his first night at Grimerth. He remembered the speech that Tompkins gave about the school building a new library underground, and he could see why they would. The current library was located in a separate building at the back of the castle and looked like it hadn't been touched by anyone in years. It was filled with overgrown plants that ran along and around the bookshelves. There were also puddles on the floor from the rain that had come in through the shattered windows, which were now letting in an unwelcome breeze.

"Are you sure we can't check out the books and do our homework back in the dorm?" said Terry, crossing his arms and closing his legs under the desk in an attempt to keep himself warm. He had already made the suggestion before they sat down, but Fergus had explained that the textbooks couldn't be checked out from the library. Apparently, there was some ancient spell put in place when the school was first founded to prevent any valuable books from being stolen. Annoyingly however, the spell also had a side effect which resulted in the library looking like the way it did now, and unfortunately, no one seemed to know how to undo the spell.

"I already told you we can't," said Fergus, busy working away in his exercise book.

It was so weird seeing the skeleton doing his homework diligently. Terry had been under the impression that Fergus was the type of person to leave work to the last minute, but in actuality, he was the type that got it out of the way first before everyone else.

"There's hardly anyone else here," said Terry, noting a couple random students here and there minding their own business.

"That's 'cause most parents bought their children the textbooks they'd need. Meanwhile, poor sods like us have to make do with these free ones from the library."

Terry picked up the open textbook in front of him to check the price printed on the back. His eyes widened when he saw the cost. "They're so expensive!" he cried.

"That's what I just said," said Fergus. "Come on, let's hurry up. I want to get out of here."

Terry sighed and made a mental note to speak to his uncle later on about buying textbooks. Right now he just needed to get his homework done.

They had two pieces of homework to complete that night. The first was from Dimples, the werewolf teacher for Curses and Cures. They had been tasked to find out the cure to being possessed by a djinn. Djinns—pronounced *jinn*—were basically invisible shape-shifting spirits. They had their own realm but could also freely venture into the human and monster realms and possess others, making them do anything they wanted. It was scary to think about, but thankfully it didn't happen very often for whatever reason.

Their second piece of homework was for Terry's uncle, the substitute teacher for History of Man and Monster until Mihai Winter returned. Terry had to write a one-page summary on Barodas, the Jackal King, an evil, grey-skinned, jackal-headed humanoid dressed like a pharaoh from ancient Egypt. He once threatened to destroy the world nearly a thousand years ago but was defeated and said to be sealed away in an eternal slumber within the black pyramids of Occulomundus. According to legend, if he were ever to be reawakened, the seven realms would never be the same again.

There was the part that really caught Terry's attention. It turned out that the Jackal King's archenemy, and the one who defeated him, was none other than Almira's forefather himself, the Spellcaster for the Ages, or as Terry now knew, Arsalan Khizaar—pronounced *Er-sull-laan Kizz-arr*—said to be the greatest spellcaster who ever lived.

It didn't take Terry and Fergus long to complete both pieces of homework, but Terry found himself wanting to read more about Almira's forefather.

"You can go on ahead," said Terry to Fergus. "I'm going to stay a bit longer."

And so two hours went by. Fergus had long since gone on ahead without Terry, and in that time, Terry had learned a number of interesting things about Arsalan Khizaar. It seemed that the great spellcaster was not a universally loved hero. There was a great amount of jealousy amongst monsters due to his unnatural power. Before his victory against the Jackal King, rumours had spread that Arsalan

Khizaar had practiced in the dark arts to enhance his strength. After the Jackal King's defeat, some suspected Arsalan Khizaar of sacrificing lives in exchange for the dark spell that had sealed the Jackal King into the black pyramids, but nothing was ever confirmed. Fearing that the Jackal King may possibly return, Arsalan Khizaar believed his powers may be needed again someday in the future, and so he sealed his strength into magic circles that could only be unlocked by those who shared his blood.

It was incredible how much Terry had learnt about Almira's ancestor from this library alone. It made him wonder if it was possible to learn about his own family history here as well. He thought back to Mihai Winter's class and what he knew from his uncle. He reasoned that there were three different categories he could search under. The first was seeing if there were any books about the Silverman family. The second was checking under the name Winter, and the third was on the Battle of New Gravespass.

There were no books on any Silverman family, but there were a few books that covered the Winter family and the Battle of New Gravespass. None of them, however, seemed to be of any relevance to Terry. Another dead end, he thought. He couldn't help but feel disappointed.

His stomach growled. He hadn't had any dinner, and it was getting late. He'd have to come back some other time.

13

Confrontation

He left the library, stretching one hand above his head and covering his yawn with the other hand as he exited the double doors.

What would have really helped Terry right now would've been some nice refreshing tomato juice to recover his stamina. Luckily for him, there was a vending machine supplying some right outside the library. In the back of Terry's mind, he found it a little strange to have vending machines scattered throughout an old fashioned place like this, but the dark colour schemes of the machines and the dim yellow lights made them blend in pretty well.

He rummaged through his trouser pocket for some spare change and pulled out a gold coin which had a skull on one side and a scythe on the other—a tribute to the Grim Reaper. In this realm, the only currency used by monsters was something called chickells. Terry had no idea what the exchange rate was for chickells to British pounds, but thankfully, he didn't have to worry about that. His uncle had taken care of all the little details like money before Terry's journey to Grimerth and bestowed him with enough chickells to last him the school year—provided he budgeted carefully. The only thing that wasn't accounted for were the textbooks, which were so ridiculously expensive that Terry would end up blowing all his money if he bought them, but that was a discussion he'd have with his uncle when he next met him.

He inserted the chickell into the slot and selected E2 for tomato juice. He was so glad that the school catered to vegetarians like himself. When he first came here, he was under the impression that being a vegetarian might be problematic in a school full of monsters, but it turned out there were quite a few other vegetarians like himself. Well, at least enough to warrant serving the option.

He watched the carton as it fell out and squatted to grab the drink after hearing the thud that followed.

"Is tomato juice really that good?"

He turned his head round to see who it was and was surprised to find Emmy standing not too far behind him with both her hands behind her back. She was wearing a black dress and a black necklace with a crimson bat shaped pendant hanging from it.

Terry felt a small lump in his throat. It was rare for pretty girls to talk to him; he wasn't used to it. He thought about Almira for a moment. Sure, Almira was pretty too, and Terry had no problem talking to her, but he reminded himself that Almira was a special case. She had been assigned to look after him and train him, so of course she would talk to him. She was his master after all, so it was perfectly normal. But Emmy, a really pretty vampire, was talking to Terry of her own accord. Well, at least as far as Terry knew. It would have been really upsetting if he found out she was also secretly hired by his uncle.

He stood up with the tomato juice carton in his hand and said, "Not really, but I've kind of gotten used to it." Terry didn't bother with the straw this time, he tore open the carton with his pointed nails and swallowed most of the juice in one go.

There was an awkward silence that followed where Emmy just stared at Terry without saying anything, watching him drink.

Terry wiped his mouth with the back of his hand. There was still a little bit of tomato juice left in the carton, he held it out towards Emmy. "You can try some if you want."

"Hmm," said Emmy finally, tapping a finger to her lips. "Maybe I should give it a try. I've heard it's actually supposed to be healthier than blood."

Terry's eyes lit up, but the moment alone between the two of them was cut short when a snobby vampire boy came through the library doors and caught them.

Kurt's eyes flicked between the two of them, and he stared at Terry with a deadly glare.

Terry froze. A memory replayed inside his head. The first night he was here, the first time he transformed … Kurt was there too! How could he have forgotten? The only class Terry shared with Kurt was PME, and Terry couldn't recall seeing him at all for the past two weeks. On top of that, with everything else that had gone on, it had completely escaped Terry that Kurt knew his secret. What a terrible oversight on Terry's part! He wondered if the snobby vampire had already told anyone, or if he was holding the information as leverage for something else his evil mind might have concocted. Whatever the case, Terry couldn't risk upsetting him at the moment. He had to play it cool, get on Kurt's good side.

Terry cleared his throat and spoke, "Everything okay, Kurt?"

Kurt didn't answer him, he just stared at Terry with a look of disgust as he cautiously moved towards Emmy. It was intense and a little awkward at the same time. Both Terry and Kurt's gazes were locked onto each other.

Kurt tried putting an arm around Emmy as casually as possible, his gaze still fixed on Terry as he did. "Come on, Emmy. Let's go," he said coolly.

Emmy stepped backwards, away from Kurt's arm. "Just what are you trying to pull here?" she said. "I'm not going anywhere with you."

But Kurt didn't listen, he broke eye contact with Terry to face Emmy and grabbed her by the wrist. "Just trust me, Emmy. You don't want to be near him, he's dangerous."

And, in that moment, Terry snapped. Maybe it was because Kurt referred to him as *dangerous* just because he was a hybrid, or maybe it was because he was trying to get Emmy to go along with him when she didn't want to. He wanted to believe it was the latter. That he was just being brave and standing up for what was right. That Kurt's words didn't hurt, didn't matter ... but they did. They really did.

"Hey! Let go of her!" Terry shouted, dropping the carton on the floor. He was careless, acting hot-headed. It was going to cost him.

Kurt saw him coming and a backhanded slap followed, knocking Terry straight onto the ground.

127

Terry gritted his teeth. He so badly wanted to transform into his wolfish form there and then to show Kurt what dangerous really was. But if he did, he'd just be proving Kurt's point.

And Emmy was still there as well, standing in shock, not sure what to do. He wondered how she would react if she knew the truth about him. Would her reaction be the same as Kurt's? He didn't want to know. He couldn't show her, couldn't let her see the real him.

Kurt crouched down to look Terry in the eyes. He whispered so that Emmy couldn't hear him. "Don't come near her again, got it? Remember, I know what you are, mongrel."

"Excuse me! What's going on here?" said a loud, familiar, and comforting voice.

Kurt jerked his head to see who had spoken.

More than halfway down from the steep stone steps that led to the back entrance of the castle was Terry's uncle, Brian Silverman.

Immediately, Kurt stood up. "Just a small misunderstanding, sir."

"I'm sure." Silverman had his hands behind his back as he approached Kurt with the look of a man who should not be crossed. "It's late," said Silverman. "Return to your dorms."

Kurt nodded his head and left. Emmy, however, looked like she wanted to stay and comfort Terry, but Silverman held up his hand to ward her back.

"I'll take care of him, my dear," said Silverman. "Go back to your dorm. It'll be time for sunrise soon, and that wouldn't be favourable for a vampire such as yourself."

***

Brian Silverman poured in a cup of hot milk tea, placing four cubes of sugar in the drink. He stirred gingerly before sliding the cup across the table and in front of Terry. He then poured himself a cup. They were both seated inside Mihai Winter's office. It was a dusty old place with no windows and cobwebs in the ceiling corners. There were also several bookshelves, a mini freezer which likely had supplies of blood stored inside for when Winter got hungry, and a small electric kettle to brew tea with—or drink hot blood, depending on your mood.

Funny how much everyone loved tea, thought Terry, watching the mist rising from his cup. In the human world, it was a universal drink loved by many like the Japanese and the Arabs, and of course, the British. Here, in the monster world as well, it seemed to be a popular drink. Perhaps due to its warm and relaxing nature. Whatever the reason, it was just nice to be drinking something different instead of the usual tomato juice. Especially since it was his uncle's tea. He always seemed to make it just right on the rare occasions they shared together.

Terry watched his uncle as he sipped his tea. He noted several bags under Silverman's eyes. The man was clearly tuckered out. On each side of the wooden desk were stacks and stacks of books and paperwork. The strain of teaching students instead of his usual line of work must have taken its toll on him. Terry had wondered how the man even had the time for teaching considering how busy his uncle normally was. Of course when he had asked, Silverman dismissed the question by saying it was nothing to worry about and that he'd taken care of it.

Why did Silverman always have to shoot down Terry's questions? Especially when it came to Terry's family. Did he think Terry wasn't old enough to handle the full story? Then again, maybe his uncle was right. Maybe Terry wasn't old enough when he thought back to what had just happened with Kurt and how Silverman had to step in to help Terry.

"I wouldn't worry about it, you know," said Silverman, setting his tea down.

"About what?"

"That vampire boy, Burt or Kurt or whatever his name is. He may know your secret, but he can't really say anything about it."

"Why not?"

"He has no proof. It's his word against yours, and you have Tompkins, the deputy headmaster, in your corner backing you up. The minotaur already spoke to the vampire boy on the night of the incident. It was also Tompkins who kept administration from looking for you when you were out of school for those three nights after your first transformation."

Terry didn't say anything in response. Despite what Silverman said, Terry still wasn't sure how much he trusted Tompkins. He didn't know why, but there was just something about the minotaur's involvement in all this that just felt out of place to him.

Terry took another sip of his tea and asked, "Has there been any update on when Mihai Winter will return?"

Silverman tilted his head to the side, crossing his arms. After a pause, he said, "No. No, not yet, but hopefully he'll be back after the Halloween festival like Tompkins said, and we can get you two acquainted then." Silverman sighed. "I'm sorry, my boy. I know you have a lot of questions, and I want to answer them, believe me, I do, but not yet. Not until the time is right."

"When will that be?"

"Believe me, you'll know. You'll know." Silverman picked up his tea to take another sip. "Now, tell me about your training."

14

A Curious Case

Terry emerged from the foliage huffing and puffing. He wasn't sure where he was, but he knew he had to make it back to the cottage if he had any hope of surviving. He ran as fast as he could.

Suddenly, a dark figure fell from the skies, crushing the ground beneath it. She lunged forward, ready to strike. Terry dodged out of the way, barely escaping with a small graze. She turned quickly, charging her fists at him. He dodged her again and watched her destroy the tree behind him.

So much power! He was surprised Almira had missed. Then he noticed her attention was divided, she wasn't directly looking at him. But why? No, there was no time to question it. This was his chance. He changed form, transforming into his darker side, the beast with no name. And feeling the raw power pulse inside him, he grabbed the witch by the neck with a single powerful hand and threw her against a tree.

She fell to the ground. He waited for her to move, but nothing happened. Had he won? Was she actually knocked out? He approached cautiously, but there was still no movement. He couldn't believe it possible; he thought for sure he wouldn't be able to defeat her so easily. He must have really caught her by surprise, and that had given him the edge. Now it was over, and he had won. He could rest easy. He reverted to his normal Terry Silverman form and went over to help her, but she'd vanished. He'd only blinked, and she was gone. Then he noticed the magic circle beneath him … but when did she have time? He turned and was greeted by a hand grabbing his face and slamming him into the ground with sheer force.

What insane strength she had. It almost made him question who the monster really was. He couldn't move. How foolish of him to transform back! If only he'd let the beast fight her, perhaps then he'd have stood a better chance.

"You're getting better," said Almira, extending a hand to help him get up.

"I've still got a long way to go," said Terry, grabbing her outstretched hand. "And you're still taking it easy on me, aren't you?" Terry dusted the dirt off his trousers with his hands once he was up.

Almira didn't answer; she only smiled. She was definitely taking it easy on him. If she had fought seriously, it would probably have been over in mere seconds.

"Someday, I'll be on the other end, picking you off the ground instead," said Terry.

Almira laughed. "In your dreams."

Terry swiped his tongue across his lips. "I need some tomato juice."

"Hold on," said Almira, she swirled her index finger in a circular motion and whispered some words. Then out of nowhere materialised a glass of tomato juice which floated in mid-air.

Terry's red eyes lit up, he reached out and grabbed the glass, gulping down the juice as fast as possible.

"Better?" she asked.

"Much. Thanks," said Terry, wiping his mouth.

Almira snapped her fingers and the now empty glass dematerialised, disappearing from Terry's hand as he watched in awe.

Terry smiled. "Shall we go back then?" He turned and headed down the pathway, only to stop after a few steps when he heard Almira call, gesturing for him to go in another direction.

"Wrong way," she said.

"I knew that," said Terry. "I was just testing you." He followed after her, watching her cloak flutter behind her as she walked. The lone soldier carrying the power of the hero who defeated the Jackal King. He didn't want to admit it, but a part of him actually admired her. Of course, if he told her that it would only boost her ego. Far better to keep it a secret.

Suddenly, Almira stumbled forward and dropped to the ground on all fours.

Terry immediately hurried to her aid, kneeling down beside her. "What happened?"

She was breathing heavy and clutching her chest. "Just give me a minute," she said. She reached down to one of her small belt pouches and pulled out a vial containing some pinkish-purple liquid. Uncapping the small container, she quickly swallowed the contents of the vial, and soon after, her breathing returned to normal. She put the empty vial back in her belt pouch, stood up, and brushed the dirt off her knees with her hands. She then continued her walk back along the path as if nothing at all had happened.

Terry stood still for a moment, confused. He rushed up to her. "What on earth was that all about?" he asked, falling in sync with her pace. "Are you okay?"

"Nothing happened," said Almira dismissively. "I'm fine."

"That was *not* nothing. Tell me what's going on."

"I told you already before, my powers are constantly changing and growing. Magic amplifies my strength, and handling all of it is a pain. That's why when I get a chance to seal some of it away, I do, but right now it's all unlocked. Seriously, don't worry. This happens about once a month, sometimes less frequently. The malaruke, which is the substance I drank, is working, controlling and balancing out the magic in my body."

Magic was so weird, thought Terry. His own knowledge of it was very limited. Before coming to the monster realm, Terry had never heard of wizards and witches using magic to amplify their strength. For that matter, up until recently, Terry had never even met a magic user, but he'd always loved reading about them and about their abilities. Almira and the rest of the Khizaar were nothing like the human spellcasters he'd read about. From what he knew, magic users came from a variety of races such as fairies, elves, djinns, and so many more. Magic itself was a universal force. It had almost unlimited potential and was a power that most craved, but it required great strength of mind and force of will to truly control.

Back when Terry was in the human realm, he had tried dabbling in a little magic himself by using a few of the old books in his uncle's old study, but he was unsuccessful to say the least. It was, therefore, all the more impressive to him that there were, for all intents and purposes, normal humans who could practice magic. And though they lacked the physical strength and endurance of monsters, they made up for it with their skills in sorcery and witchcraft. And yet, here was Almira, a descendant of the Spellcaster for the Ages. Someone who defied the norm. Someone who could break trees with her fists, who didn't need a wand or ring to practise magic, and could keep up with the biggest monsters, even putting some of them to shame. It made him wonder just what her limits were exactly and how powerful she would be once she was an adult.

Lola, Almira's pet cockatiel, swooped in and landed on Terry's shoulder. Lola was a lively bird, and recently, she'd taken a liking to Terry which seemed to make Almira a little jealous. He noticed a small tube had been secured around her neck, like something a carrier pigeon would have. The bird rubbed herself against his neck. Terry smiled and petted the little creature lovingly. "What's this tube thing on her?" he asked.

"That's for me," said Almira, approaching them both looking slightly irritated. "Lola," she said in a tone that was almost like a mother calling her daughter. "You got my paper?"

Lola bowed her head, and Almira removed the tube. She then petted the bird and gave a brief smile. "Good job. Now listen, there was a spy following us moments ago. You'll know him when you see him. Can you go deal with him, please?"

The bird straightened up and raised a wing to her head, like a soldier saluting their superior. She then flew off into the direction that they'd just left.

"A spy? What spy? What are you talking about?" asked Terry.

"Your vampire friend, Kurt. I noticed him tailing us during our sparring session. I'm sure he's taken some pictures of you transforming."

Terry's heart sank. If what Almira had said was true, then that would mean Kurt had gotten the proof he'd needed to expose Terry. "We have to go after him!" Terry cried.

"Calm down," said Almira, walking ahead without a care in the world. "Lola's on it."

"What do you mean she's on it? What's a cockatiel going to do to a freaking vampire?"

"She doesn't need to do anything to him," said Almira without stopping. "She just needs to break or steal his camera, both of which should be easy enough for her."

"Are you sure?"

Almira stopped and turned to face him. "Terry, do you trust me?"

Terry hesitated for a moment. He did trust her, more than he cared to admit actually, but he didn't want to say it, so he nodded instead.

"Good," said Almira. "Now let's head back, shall we?" She opened the tube in her hand and pulled out what looked like a mini rolled up newspaper. Licking her index finger, she tapped the paper. Suddenly, it expanded into a regular sized newspaper. On the front page was a story about an UGOM official going missing. Almira opened the paper, reading it while walking. "Huh! Oh, I see! Hmm! How curious!" she exclaimed. "How very curious, indeed!"

"What? What is it?" said Terry.

"Oh, nothing. Just that the Demon Wolf's patterns have changed."

"Fergus says all they ever talk about on the news is the Demon Wolf."

Almira stopped and lowered her paper to look at Terry. "Have you ever read the news?"

"No, why would I read the newspaper? Isn't that for old people?"

Almira rolled up the newspaper and whacked Terry on the head with it.

"Ouch! What was that for?" he said, rubbing his head.

"For being an ignoramus," said Almira before continuing to walk again. "Now listen, unless you actually follow the news, you can't really form an opinion on it. Got it?"

Terry nodded.

"Yes, the Demon Wolf gets a lot of coverage, but that's 'cause he attracts the most attention. Curiosity draws us to him. He's an enigma waiting to be solved. Once we know everything about him, he'll be old news."

"How do you know it's a he?"

"Well, we don't. Everyone just assumes it. There's never been many clues or evidence left behind, but for the first time in a long time, we finally have something new to go on. A real lead in the investigation."

"You sound really interested in this case. Almost sounds like you're a detective. A magical witch detective," said Terry, finding the notion absurdly amusing.

"You laugh, but you know I can beat you up."

"Is there anything you're bad at?"

"Sure, I can fight, but that's just 'cause I've been trained since I was a child and forced to survive in harsh conditions. Also, I never said I was a detective or that I was good at detective work, so don't go thinking I'm some teen private eye or anything. I just like reading up on cases and learning about them. There's a certain thrill to it, you know?"

"So, you've never considered trying to solve a case on your own?"

Almira raised an eyebrow. "Why? You interested in solving the mystery of the Demon Wolf? Do you honestly think UGOM's goblins wouldn't have thought of whatever we'd come up with?"

Terry shrugged his shoulders. "Lay it on me," he said. "Goblins think differently from us. We might come up with another angle they haven't considered."

"Don't underestimate how cunning a goblin can be. But, whatever, I guess theorising couldn't hurt," said Almira with a sigh. "Okay, so in the past, the Demon Wolf's victims have always been random. There was never a connection between any of them. The only thing in common was that all of their bodies had been mutated with wolf genes, causing them to transform into demonic half-wolves before they were killed."

"Right, Fergus told me about that. He also said that a werewolf bite kills their victims, so they don't transform others into wolves themselves. Is that right?"

"Pretty much, but that's assuming that the Demon Wolf is actually a normal werewolf, which we can rule out 'cause no normal werewolf could kill some of the monsters the Demon Wolf has killed. Also, they've never found any bite marks on any of the victims, so it wouldn't have been a result of being bitten anyway."

"But then how do they transform?"

"That's still a mystery. There are some theories but nothing conclusive."

"All right, what else you got?"

"In the past, the Demon Wolf would pick his victims at random, but there's been a new wave of attacks that have taken place in the last two weeks, which all seem to be targeting specific monsters. All of the recent victims have been either UGOM officials or hospital staff."

"Why go after them?"

"Who knows? The media haven't said, but my guess is that he's searching for something. I mean, why else target these particular people? Besides, this time not all the victims are being transformed into half-wolves ... some are being killed without a transformation."

"Then how do we know it's the same Demon Wolf?"

"The injuries caused by the Demon Wolf are unique. All the victims have similar lacerations across the chest. Also, no known creature has the physical strength to ..." She stopped abruptly.

"What is it?" said Terry, following her eyes.

Almira held up her hand for silence. After a while, Terry heard it too. Not far off were the faint sounds of approaching footsteps and voices mumbling. Almira signalled Terry to hide. They moved quietly and crouched behind the trees. Soon after, Tompkins and Silverman came into view, appearing to be deep in conversation.

Terry sighed in relief and was about to reveal himself but was yanked back by Almira. She held her index finger up to her lips.

"Understand that my hands were tied," said Tompkins, his voice noticeably low as though he was cautious of eavesdroppers.

Silverman didn't look happy. In fact, Terry thought his uncle looked rather annoyed. "How long have you known he was in the hospital?"

"A few weeks now. A couple of hours after the incident occurred."

"And we can't visit him?"

"Only the headmistress and the Prime President himself are allowed to see him."

Silverman paused and cocked his head. "The Prime President? Surely you jest! Why would the high and mighty Snark Dia concern himself with some lowly vampire?"

"It seems this incident goes beyond a simple attack, my friend. UGOM believes it may be connected to the Demon Wolf. Mihai Winter is the only person to survive an encounter with the creature, hence they insist there should be the highest level of protection in case the Demon Wolf returns."

Terry and Almira exchanged glances with each other, eyes wide. They dared not move, remaining silent and continuing to listen.

"I see," said Silverman, rubbing his chin. "So, they need him alive for questioning."

"Indeed, and with the recent change in killings, it's clear the Demon Wolf is looking to finish the job. Winter is comatose at present, but when he awakens, he may hold the answer to finally putting an end to this nightmare."

"You mustn't mention this to the boy. I don't wish for him to worry."

Tompkins nodded in agreement, and they continued to walk on together.

Terry looked at Almira. This was huge news.

Once Tompkins and Silverman had left, Almira led Terry straight to the cottage and unrolled a map of the island onto the table. She began plotting out where the attacks had taken place. Both new and old, they all seemed to have occurred away from Grimerth and were concentrated more towards the village of Grimdale near the black pyramids and the watchtower. But there was one thing Terry couldn't place: where exactly was the hospital? He was about to ask Almira, but before he had a chance, Tompkins had returned. He knocked on the door and, without waiting for an answer, walked in. Almira instinctively tried hiding the map, but she wasn't fast enough.

"Please, don't tell me you're looking into the Demon Wolf again?" said Tompkins with heavy eyes and arms akimbo. "How many times have I told you to leave it to UGOM?"

"I was just showing Terry where the Halloween festival is taking place," lied Almira, pushing the map into Terry's arms.

Nice save, thought Terry. He rolled up the map. "That's right, sir. Since I'm new to the island, I asked Almira if she had a map to help me navigate my way around Grimdale."

"I see. Well, just ensure you keep away from the outskirts, and you should be fine. Speaking of Halloween," said Tompkins, now addressing Almira. "You and the other prefects are required to attend the meeting in preparation for the festivities."

"Ugh. Not another meeting," said Almira rolling her eyes. "I should never have taken your advice to become a prefect."

"To be honest, I'm still surprised you agreed."

Almira shrugged. "Eh, what can I say? I like the authority it gives me."

15

Halloween Festival

"So, let me get this straight," said Fergus as he sat down with Terry the next night during lunch. "You and the witch are playing detectives now? And *why* wasn't I invited?"

"Is that all you took away from what I just told you?" asked Terry.

Fergus rubbed his chin thoughtfully. "Yes," he confessed. "But there's one thing I don't get. Weren't you studying under Almira? How did you guys go from trying to tame the wolf inside you to trying to solve a case that even UGOM themselves can't solve?"

Terry wondered about that for a moment. To Almira, it was probably just pure curiosity, but for himself, it was more personal now that he knew his grandfather's life was at stake.

"And you didn't tell your uncle or Tompkins that you overheard them?" asked Fergus.

"No. Almira says it's best we keep it between ourselves. Besides, my uncle doesn't want me to know. If I say anything, he'll be more on his guard than he already is, and I know from experience how secretive he can be," said Terry, poking his food with his fork. He wasn't able to eat. It was strange, he didn't really know Mihai Winter at all, but he still couldn't help feeling concerned. After all, Winter and his uncle were the only family Terry had, and at the end of the night, family was family, regardless of history.

"And Almira can't help us 'cause she's busy with prefect duties?"

"Pretty much, but I can't just sit by and wait for this Demon Wolf to kill my grandfather. I must do something. If we can find him, we might be able to stop him."

"This is crazy. You're crazy. We're not the police. We're just kids and you want to go looking for a creature that scares even the biggest monsters?"

Terry forced a grin, putting up false bravado. "I'm a wolfpire, Fergus. You said it yourself, I'm the worst wolf. So what if he's a demon? I've gone toe-to-toe with Almira, and she can knock trees down with her fists. Next to her, this creature is nothing."

"You are so brave," said Fergus admiringly, taking a sip from his glass of milk which leaked right through him as usual. "What would you like me to put on your tombstone?"

"Ha-ha. Take a look at this." Terry unzipped his backpack and removed the map he was given by Almira. "Last night Almira mapped out where the attacks had taken place. She said it was something called geographic profiling or whatever. I think it's basically a fancy way of saying you're tracking the perpetrator by using the location of their crimes to find out where they live. Anyway, I thought about it and noticed something. All the attacks happen in the northwest area, where the cemetery, watchtower, and black pyramids are."

"But UGOM's goblins have already searched those areas and found nothing."

"It can't hurt for us to have a go at it," said Terry, rolling up the map and putting it away. "I'm guessing the Halloween festival will be our only opportunity to visit Grimdale since we aren't normally allowed outside of Grimerth or the dorms."

"That's right, the main festival is in Grimdale."

"Things might get dangerous. Are you with me?" said Terry, extending a hand.

"Do I have a choice?" Fergus returned the gesture, gripping Terry's hand firmly.

***

"While I'm sure you're all excited about the festival," said the voice of Reason, the invisible tutor, while standing most likely at the front of the bus as they journeyed to Grimdale, "the headless headmistress has stressed that you all maintain a level head. As if she's one to talk, right? Anyway, once we arrive at Grimdale, you'll all be free to do whatever you want, but I expect everyone to be on their best behaviour. If you're caught doing something stupid, you'll be taken straight back to the castle and detained until the night is over. With that said, remember to have fun and be sensible. I wish you all a pleasant night."

Before they all reached the festival, they were placed into groups of three on the bus. The idea was that everyone would be with someone and not wander off alone. Terry was not a fan of forced socialising. Fortunately, he at least had Fergus in his group.

The village of Grimdale was alive with lights and music. As Terry left the bus, he was welcomed by loud organ music and the smell of burnt crispy beetles and mice heads on sticks. Laughter and chatter filled the night air. At the entrance was a decaying clown zombie, welcoming everyone inside with free balloons. Behind him were a variety of attractions. Some normal looking, like a hall of mirrors and haunted houses. Others not so much, like the giant hairy spider that would spin around after monsters hopped onto its legs, or the zombie bumper cars where blood would spurt out whenever they bumped together.

As his eyes wandered about, a peculiar contraption caught Terry's attention. A small child that looked like a mini version of Frankenstein's monster ran up to one of the rusty fortune teller machines designed like a mechanical old witch and inserted a coin inside. Soon after, a small printed sheet spurted out, and the child read it with bubbling joy only to find himself in tears after he'd finished reading the apparent sinister prediction. He cried out for his mother who rushed from the crowd to cradle him.

"Wow, I wonder what it said?" said Emmy.

"Let's go try it out," said Fergus.

Terry pulled the skeleton to one side and whispered fiercely, "What are you doing? Did you forget what we're here for? We can't waste time."

"Calm down. It's important to improvise. We'll distract her with some games, and then we'll sneak off. Now let's see what our fortunes tell us."

Each of them took turns inserting coins and retrieving fortunes.

Fergus was up first, his fortune read:

MILK IS GOOD FOR YOUR BONES.

Fergus nodded approvingly. "It really knows its stuff."

"It doesn't seem to know that you can't drink it," replied Terry, "and that it never reaches your bones."

"What do you mean, I can't?" said Fergus, aghast.

Terry rolled his eyes in exasperation.

"I'm going next." Emmy ran up to the machine, inserted a coin, and tore off her fortune.

BLOOD IS NEARBY TO YOU.

"Wow, this thing really is spot on," she said. Her red lined eyes glowed even redder than usual.

Terry looked irritated. "These are the worst fortunes I've ever seen." Still, he supposed there was no harm in seeing what his fortune would say. He pulled out a coin and rubbed it for luck before slotting it into the machine. Small sparks erupted from the electronic old witch and her eyes lit up, eyeing Terry furiously. She cackled mechanically, and a moment later, a half-burnt piece of paper spurted out. Terry exchanged a glance with the others, and they all shrugged in confusion. He pulled out what remained of the fortune cautiously and read it.

—AL. DEATH.

What was that supposed to mean? Terry wondered. He stared at the words in confusion as a strange sense of dread crept over him.

Emmy seemed to have noticed Terry's expression. "I wouldn't worry about it, Terry. Fortunes are a load of rubbish anyway. You saw what we all got."

Fergus placed his bony fingers on Terry's shoulder as if to comfort him. "Put me in your will."

"No way," said Terry flatly, crumpling up the fortune and throwing it away.

"Hey, let's go check out the haunted house!" said Emmy.

Fergus leaned close to Terry and whispered, "This will be the perfect way to ditch her. We can pretend to get super scared while we're inside and then run out screaming."

"You mean like a couple of cowards?" said Terry. "Won't that ruin my reputation?"

"Not that you had any reputation to begin with. But, hey, if you stop the Demon Wolf, we'll be legends, so it'll all balance out in the end."

That was a big if, but he couldn't let Fergus know he was worried. Terry felt the blood drain from his face. Another problem presented itself when he saw the haunted house. He remembered he hated haunted houses. The lack of light, strange voices whispering in his ear and weird creatures touching his face. No, thank you. Terry wanted none of it. But wait, wasn't that a good thing? At least this way he wouldn't have to pretend to be afraid.

"What's wrong?" said Emmy. "Don't tell me you're a chicken."

Terry eyed her with amusement. He couldn't believe the same old trick was being used in the monster world too. Sometimes this world was a little too similar to home. "I'll have you know that's a very common misconception," said Terry. "Chickens are actually rather brave animals."

Emmy snorted. "So, are you telling me that a chicken is braver than you?"

"Well, no, that's not what I said." He found himself struggling for a comeback with the limited words his brain could muster.

"Come on." Emmy grabbed his hand and pulled him inside the haunted house.

Terry tried protesting, but Emmy had a firm grip, and within seconds, he was plunged into darkness. Not good. He couldn't see a blasted thing. How was he supposed to find his way out? He held onto Emmy's hand as they wandered through the black void. Then he heard a sinister laugh.

Terry shrieked. "What was that?"

"Not sure," said Emmy. "There's nothing around, just empty cells. Looks like a prison."

"Wait, you can see what's around us?"

"For the most part. Why? Can't you?"

"No. All I see is darkness."

Emmy stood still and looked at him. "Really? You can't see anything?"

Terry shook his head. "Nope."

"Ah, I guess since you're a day vampire, your night vision isn't so good. Well, no worries, just don't let go of my hand. I'll keep you safe."

A blood-curdling scream immediately followed, making Terry jump.

Oh no, no, no. This was getting way out of hand. He had to leave fast. *Hello?* He felt something cold and hard crawl up his leg. He screamed, "Something's on me! Help! Get it off, GET IT OFF! GET IT OFF!"

"Calm down!" said Emmy. "I'll get it!"

But Terry couldn't stay still. He pushed a hand down his trousers and pulled out whatever was crawling up him, throwing it as far as possible. Then came a second one, this time crawling down his neck. He yelled, grabbing whatever it was and hurling it. There was a hiss in the darkness. Without thinking, he ran, breaking free from Emmy's grip. His heart in his throat, fear had taken command of his body. He emerged from the haunted house and found himself back at the festival, finally surrounded by lights again. He sighed in relief, then gasped, the realisation of how weak and pathetic he must have looked in front of Emmy quickly dawning on him. Ugh, he was never going to live this down, was he?

"That worked better than I thought it would," said Fergus, putting a bony hand on Terry's shoulder. "Sorry about the scare, mate, but I wish you hadn't thrown my left hand so hard."

"That was you?" said Terry. "You jerk! You nearly gave me a heart attack!"

The skeleton rattled. "We better move quickly or else Emmy will catch up to us."

Fergus was right. There was work to be done, and it had to be done fast before anyone caught on.

"What? What is it?" said Terry, as he felt Fergus's elbow poke his arm.

"Look over there." Fergus gestured towards a suspicious looking Basil Tompkins. The minotaur seemed to be moving away from the festival, wary of any onlookers.

"What do you think he's up to?" said Fergus.

"Not sure, looks like he's heading in the same direction as us. Let's follow him."

16

The Demon's Dwellings

I t became increasingly foggier the further Terry and Fergus got towards the edge of the town. Were they near the black pyramids? Or was it the cemetery? It was difficult to discern. The mist had now engulfed them entirely, leaving them completely alone with no sign of Tompkins anywhere. Soon, even the sounds from the lively festival began to dissolve, and it became all too eerily silent. For a while they roamed around aimlessly, attempting to gain their bearings.

"I can't see anything," said Fergus.

"That's 'cause you don't have any eyes," said Terry, though this was hardly the time for him to be making jokes.

Through the mist appeared a gravestone, and then slowly behind it appeared an entire cemetery watched over by a lifelike statue of the Grim Reaper. He was a charcoal skeletal figure, dressed in a black cloak with his hood on and his bony hands held out openly, almost like a beggar. Or perhaps, more accurately, as though offering a prayer for the dead.

Terry couldn't quite place his finger on it, but there was something familiar about this place. It was almost as if he had seen it before somewhere, like in a dream. He could feel a tug in his heart drawing him closer to the gravestones and the personification of death.

"AAAGGGHHH!" cried Fergus, his voice coming from a distance and followed by a loud thud.

Terry spun round and called out for the skeleton. There was silence. He shouted again.

"Down here!" echoed Fergus's voice from a wishing well to the side of a gravestone.

Terry moved towards the source and peered inside, but he was unable to make anything out except a dark pit.

"Fergus? How'd you get down there?"

"How do you think I did? I tripped, you fool! I wasn't paying attention and stumbled. Anyway, forget that, I need you to climb down and help me out. I can't put myself back together again if I can't see where my bones are."

Terry grabbed the thick rope that was attached to the well. For some reason there was no bucket, so he made do with the rope and lowered it, ensuring that it was secure. "Do you see the rope?" he shouted.

"Just about."

"I'm coming down." The descent was daunting. Terry held onto the rope firmly and climbed down cautiously, placing a foot either side of the walls of the well as he lowered himself. He was reminded of the first time he met Almira and how he had to pass through that dark, claustrophobic door. God, how empty and cold that felt. It was the same here, only this time instead of going towards the light, he was moving away from it.

"Ouch! Watch it! You're stepping on my foot!"

"Oops, sorry," said Terry, letting go off the rope. "I can't see a thing here."

"Just feel around for my bones and bring them closer to me. I can do the rest myself."

"This is so confusing," said Terry.

"What's confusing about picking up bones?"

"I'm talking about the well. Normally they have water in them, but there's none here. I'd assume it's a dried out well, but then I would expect there to be a muddy hole, which there isn't. Feels more like normal ground. Also, there was no bucket either. Just what kind of well is this?"

"Who cares?" said Fergus. "Are you going to give me a hand or not?"

"Right. Sorry." Piece by piece, bone by bone, Terry slowly helped Fergus put himself back together again.

"Almost there. I just need my elbow joint."

"Hold on." Terry shuffled his hands around on the ground. He stopped, feeling something hard and cold, almost like a bone, but there was something odd about it. Was it damaged? He grabbed onto it and tried picking it up, but it didn't move. Was it stuck? He tried again. Then something happened. Something incredible. The ground began to move.

"What did you do?" said Fergus, his voice trembling in fear. "What's going on?"

"It's almost like we're in an elevator," said Terry, realising he must have pulled some kind of lever as they were descending lower and lower underground. Soon there was light, but by God, did he wish there wasn't, for this new light revealed nothing but terror.

He stood motionless in horror, unable to believe his eyes. Before him were cages and cages of dead bodies. Half werewolf creatures, each mutilated and destroyed. He turned his face away, unable to stare at the dreadful sight much longer.

Something caught his eye. Lying on the floor were several syringes. "So that's how he transforms his victims," said Terry, crouching down to pick one up. "He injects them."

"It stinks down here," said Fergus. He'd found his missing elbow and was now whole once more. "Dear God," he whispered upon seeing the bodies. "All these rotting corpses. I've always read about it, but seeing it is completely different. Poor sods. How can anyone do this?"

"It's Tompkins," said Terry. "He's the Demon Wolf. I'm sure of it."

"What makes you so sure?"

Terry stood up. "Just look where following him led us."

"That's a big stretch. We were going to search here anyway. It was one of the locations you mapped out with that geo detective work stuff you were doing."

"But why else would he head this way?"

"Why haven't we found him here then?" said Fergus, not entirely convinced. "We lost him ages ago. He could have gone anywhere."

"Where else is there to go?" said Terry, certain that he was correct. "He must have already gotten what he wanted and left. Think about it, who's going to suspect a minotaur to be the Demon Wolf? No one! It's the perfect cover! He also told Almira to back off from the case. Why would he do that unless he was hiding something? You know, I never trusted that guy from the start. He knew about my grandfather being hospitalised, and then when my uncle found out about it, Tompkins must have panicked and decided to use this as an opportunity to finish the job. He must have come here to grab a syringe and is probably planning to use it on Winter as we speak. We've got to get out of here and find Almira so we can stop him!"

"I really think you're jumping to conclusions here. And why do you need Almira? I thought you said you could take him on your own?"

"Have you seen those guys?" said Terry, pointing to the disfigured carcases. "No way am I going to stand a chance against someone who can do that. We need Almira."

17

Approaching Darkness

Back at the festival, they were greeted by Emmy, who suddenly locked arms with Terry. "Found you!" she said cheerfully with a big grin plastered across her face. "Come on, let's go on the Ferris wheel."

"That sounds like fun. Can I come?" said Fergus.

"Bugger off, bone head," said Emmy.

Under normal circumstances, Terry might have been happy for a date with Emmy, because she was after all one of the prettiest vampires he'd ever seen, but this was so not the right time. He had to find Almira and stop Tompkins, and he had to do it fast. Lives were at stake! Wait, couldn't this work to Terry's advantage as well? He considered the situation. If he was on the Ferris wheel with Emmy, then he'd have a bird's eye view of everything. He'd be able to spot Almira and Tompkins in an instant. Yes, it could totally work! Oh, but this was going to be a challenge for someone like him who hated heights.

Before he knew it, he was on the Ferris wheel with Emmy and Fergus—the skeleton just wouldn't take no for an answer, so Emmy had no choice but to let him on.

Terry could feel his stomach churn as the cart started moving. Ugh, this was not going to be fun. He steadied himself, avoiding looking down at the ground, silently praying that he would be okay.

Emmy was strangely quiet the entire time, her attention focused on what was below. Was she also afraid of heights? Terry wondered.

Fergus noticed and attempted to offer some comfort as he slowly moved himself closer to her inside the abnormally spacious cart and clanked his bony arm around her shoulders.

"What are you doing?" asked Emmy, backing away in confusion by the skeleton's actions.

It was mildly entertaining to watch and somehow gave Terry a bit more confidence about looking below. He was just about ready to look when the cart came to a halt and the abrupt jerk caused him to lose balance and fall over inside the cart as it swung back and forth. He picked himself up and anxiously peered outside for signs of Almira or Tompkins. A sudden spell of dizziness overpowered him. They'd stopped right at the top. Why? They were so high up. Terry put his hand to his heart and closed his eyes. Deep breaths. Deep breaths.

"Seems the power is out," said Emmy.

"Yeah, looks like it," Terry laughed nervously. "I wonder what's wrong." He slowly backed away from the view and heard the sudden sound of someone's bones clattering. Terry turned and was greeted with a fist to the face. He fell with a loud thud, causing the cart to rock. Warm blood filled his mouth. Before he could pick himself up, he received a kick to the stomach. "W—what are you doing?" he said, turning to look Emmy in the eyes.

She stared at him with malicious glee. "Because you're dangerous and I hate you," she said, lifting her foot and bringing it down on his face.

Terry felt his nose crack under the pressure and grimaced in pain. Once Emmy's foot lifted, he found Kurt standing in her place. For a moment, his brain stopped working, as if time had come to a standstill. What was going on? He looked at Fergus, who'd been gagged with a cloth and restrained with multiple belts in the corner of the cart, and then back to Kurt. He wiped the blood from his nose and picked himself up slowly. "Kurt? What are you doing here?"

Kurt looked at him with a confused expression. Then he shook his head and launched himself onto Terry with both hands, grabbing Terry's neck and shaking him violently. "Transform!" he yelled, like some demented madman.

Transform? Why? Terry couldn't help but feel confused. If Kurt was trying to get him to expose himself, why wait till they were alone on a Ferris wheel? Why not just attack him in public? And more importantly, just how long had Kurt been disguised as Emmy? Eww, just the thought that he'd been hanging out with Kurt instead of Emmy made him shudder, but he couldn't think about it anymore, his eyes were about to burst out of their sockets. He was struggling to breathe and had to find a way out. He thrust his lower body upwards, causing Kurt to release the grip on his throat. Using the moment to his advantage, he gave Kurt a shove, and as he fell over, he pinned him to the bottom of the cart.

"What did you do with Emmy?" he demanded.

Kurt raised his hand and pointed in the direction behind Terry. He turned to check but soon realised, he'd made a mistake. Idiot! He'd been fooled with the oldest trick in the book. Kurt seized the opportunity and grabbed Terry by the collar with his right hand, shifting his weight to the right and throwing Terry to the side. Before Terry could get up to fight back, Kurt picked him up and hurled him against the cart door, knocking it open.

Terry grunted. His head was hanging outside the door as he stared down at the view below. A burst of wooziness overpowered him, but he pushed himself upwards, pausing midway. In the watchtower nearby, through the open window, he could see a familiar figure: Mihai Winter, lying unconscious in a bed with several tubes attached to him. Approaching him was none other than Basil Tompkins!

A sharp pain pierced Terry's shoulder and he yelled out in agony. Something had been lodged inside him, and the next thing he knew, he was being forced out of the cart. He tried turning in an attempt to stop Kurt, but it was too late, and he was now hanging from the open door with only a single hand saving him from falling. He stared at Kurt who was standing above him, ready to send Terry plummeting to his death.

"Are you actually trying to kill me?" said Terry breathlessly. "I know you hate me, but isn't this going a bit too far?"

"I can't believe you fell for the same trick twice," said Kurt. "You really are an idiot. I thought the skeleton might hinder my plans, but he's as useless as ever. Now transform, you mongrel. You won't die in your beast form."

"Why do you want me to transform so much?" Terry already knew the answer to this question, but he found himself asking anyway.

"Simple, the moment you do, you'll be exposed to the entire world and ruined forever. Emmy will finally see you for the disgusting mutt you really are. You'll have nowhere to hide, you filthy half-breed. Now shut up and transform."

This was exactly what Silverman had warned Terry about. If Kurt succeeded in exposing Terry's secret, then he really would be ruined. He'd have nowhere to go, nowhere to call home. Terry's grip loosened. Whatever Kurt had stabbed into his shoulder with was beginning to really sting. "What if I refuse to transform?" he said.

"Ha, then you'll be killing yourself," said Kurt. "I know half your brain is a mongrel's, but even you're not that stupid, are you?"

There had to be a way out of this. If Kurt had really wanted Terry dead, he wouldn't have gone through an elaborate scheme like this. His only goal was to have Terry transform. He didn't plan to kill him, so there was definitely a line he wasn't willing to cross. "I'll leave my fate in your hands," said Terry with so much confidence that even he believed it himself.

Kurt hesitated. "You're bluffing," he said, trying to read Terry's expression.

Terry grinned. "Wanna bet on it? It's only the life of a mongrel after all." He could see the restraint in Kurt's face. It was taking all his willpower to hold himself back from bringing his foot down on Terry, and for an instant, Terry wondered if Kurt might just kill him. Then Kurt sighed, taking his foot away from Terry's hand, but as he did, the cart jerked again and he lost his balance, falling out of the door. Someone must have attempted to restart the Ferris wheel but failed. Kurt was now hanging in mid-air and only Terry's grip was saving him from falling to his untimely demise.

A crowd had taken notice and gathered below, murmuring amongst themselves and calling for help.

"Oh God! Oh God!" yelled Kurt. "Please, I don't want to die!" He eyed the view below him. "This wasn't part of the plan. Darn it, where the heck is that stupid Yohan?"

Terry grimaced. "Stop squirming," he commanded. He tried mustering what strength he could to pull Kurt up, but the pain in his shoulders only got worse. He could feel his strength slipping away. He wouldn't be able to hold on much longer. He needed to transform.

"Let go of me."

Terry looked down at Kurt with surprise. "I'm sorry, what?"

"You heard me, let go."

"Didn't you just say you didn't want to die?"

"No, idiot. Let go of me so I can climb up you instead. I can't allow myself to be in debt to a half-breed. Once your hand is free, get a better grip, and no matter what you do, don't fall. Got it?"

Terry loosened his grip on Kurt's hand, and Kurt firmly grabbed onto Terry's legs, causing Terry to almost completely lose his grip. "Careful!" He managed to still hold on somehow. "Hurry up," Terry grunted.

Kurt pulled himself up using Terry as support and made his way back into the cart. He then grabbed Terry and helped him in. For a moment, they both sat there, panting with exhaustion, sitting across from one another in silence with only the sound of rasping breaths between them.

"Turn around," said Kurt.

"Why?" said Terry, too tired to move.

Kurt dragged himself towards Terry and reached behind him to pull out the item that he'd lodged in his shoulder.

Terry yelled in pain. "What is that?" he asked, feeling his strength return. The wound on his shoulder felt like it was instantaneously closing.

"A silverwood stake," said Kurt, tossing the small object to Terry. "Fatal to half-breeds like you. Small quantities like that will nullify your healing and reduce your strength. If I really wanted you dead, I would have stuck it through your heart, but then I'd have the goblins and Tompkins after me."

Terry inspected the silver stake, which must have been around five inches long. Incredible craftsmanship, he thought. It looked just like a wooden stake, even detailed with engravings like one, and it felt just like real wood, but the colour was a unique silver instead of brown. It didn't look like paint, it appeared as if the wood was naturally that colour.

"Where did you get it?" Terry asked.

"My father is an avid collector of strange items," said Kurt. "He's got all sorts of odd stuff like dragon nails and fairy dust. He's given me a lot of random things for my birthdays. Never really used any of them, just kept them stored in a junk box."

"Why are you telling me this?"

"First, tell me why you saved me," said Kurt.

"I don't know," said Terry. He wondered if he should have said something profound instead, but the truth was he just felt it was the right thing to do.

Kurt's head fell, he was staring at the floor. How strange it must have been for him to try ruining someone only to be saved by them.

This was Terry's chance. He silently put the silverwood stake away safely into the inner breast pocket of his blazer. No way was Terry going to hand something so deadly back to someone like Kurt. "What did you do with the real Emmy? Is she okay?"

"She's fine. Never laid a finger on her."

Terry sighed. Knowing Emmy hadn't been harmed because of him was a relief. "How'd you disguise yourself as her anyway?" he asked.

"Had a little help from Yohan with his magic," said Kurt. "Spell must have worn off when I kicked you. That lazy, useless elf only knows about five spells, and he can't even get those right half the time."

Terry noticed poor Fergus sitting in the corner still tied up and went over to free him.

"Finally!" cried Fergus. "I thought I was going to suffocate." He then turned to Kurt. "You! How dare you tie me up like that?"

The lights came on and the Ferris wheel began to move again. "There's something else I've actually been meaning to ask you," said Terry, holding Fergus back.

"What's that?" said Kurt.

"Why'd you call me dangerous? Are hybrids really that much of a threat to you?"

Kurt regarded Terry thoughtfully and then, after some consideration, finally spoke. "Do you really believe that you can control that beast inside you?"

"Well, if you hadn't noticed, I'm controlling it just fine right now," said Terry.

Kurt scoffed. "You're fooling yourself."

"Why? I didn't transform when you tried forcing my hand only moments ago. I even held myself back that night you smacked me down in front of Emmy, and believe me, that night I really did want to transform and show you what I could do."

"Hybrids like you are no better than the Demon Wolf," said Kurt. "You'll see. That beast may be listening to you now, but what happens when it finally realises it doesn't need you? There'll come a time where you won't be able to contain it anymore, and when that happens, the beast will eat you from the inside. All that'll be left is a rabid dog looking to be put down."

Terry clenched his fists but refrained from saying anything in response.

"If that's really how you feel, then why didn't you just let Terry fall?" asked Fergus.

"I'm not a killer, that's why. I just wanted the world to see him for what he truly is, a mongrel pretending to be a vampire." Kurt's eyes flicked to Terry. "Let me make this clear … nothing changes between us. I will never be friends with a half-breed like you, but that said, you did just save my life tonight after I nearly cost you yours. For that, I'll spare your secret."

"Thank you," said Terry, relaxing his fists.

"Don't get carried away. Once we leave this cart, we're enemies again. Got it?"

Terry nodded.

"Also, tell your witch friend she owes me a camera. Her stupid pet bird broke mine, and if my father finds out, then he's going to kill me."

"I'll be sure she gets the message," said Terry, making a mental note to buy some bird seed to thank Lola with later on.

"Speaking of Almira, do you know where she is?" asked Fergus.

Terry gestured for Fergus to come closer and whispered, "We don't have time to find her anymore. I saw Tompkins when the Ferris wheel stopped. He's in the watchtower and he's about to kill Winter. We've got to get there now, or it may be too late."

***

At the entrance of the watchtower, hovering upside-down on a broomstick and looking bored out of her mind, was none other than Almira. "What are you two doing here?" she asked, rotating herself upwards. She climbed off her broom, which then dematerialised into nothing, as though it had never been there.

"Us? What about you?" said Fergus.

"Prefect duties. I'm to stop anyone from going inside this building behind me."

"We don't have a lot of time," said Terry, cutting in. "We need to get inside and stop Tompkins. He's about to kill Winter!"

"Whoa, slow down," said Almira, holding up a hand in protest and blocking their path. "Tompkins was asked by the headmistress to look after Winter. He's not going to kill him."

"You're wasting time! Just let me through, and I'll prove it to you."

"All right! Fine!" Almira rolled her eyes, lowered her hand and stepped aside. "Let's go. He's on the fourteenth floor, third room to your right."

They all sped off, running down corridors and climbing up stairs. It was eerily silent and empty throughout the building. There seemed to be no one present. Terry ran up another flight of stairs as fast as he could with Fergus and Almira following behind him. He prayed he wasn't too late and that Winter had somehow woken up at the last second to defend himself. He reached for the handle and swung the door open.

There lay Mihai Winter with a stake pierced right through his heart, and the man standing beside him with blood-soaked hands wasn't Basil Tompkins, but his uncle, Brian Silverman.

18

For Whom You Never Knew

"Well, well, well!" said Silverman upon seeing Terry and his cohorts enter the poorly lit room. "I must confess, I'm rather surprised to find you here, my boy. This does complicate matters for me, but I suppose all good things must eventually come to an end."

Terry was at a loss, unable to speak. His mind failed him, incapable of fully processing the situation. On the floor lay an unconscious Tompkins with claw marks across his chest. Almira rushed to his aid, and Fergus joined her.

Silverman smiled. "Caught with my hand in the cookie jar, how embarrassing," he said without any delicacy. "It is somewhat humorous, though. I've been getting away with murder for so many years, and after all my careful planning, I slip up and get caught like this. How dreadful! How utterly dreadful!" Silverman continued in mock exasperation. "Strange how life works sometimes, don't you agree, my boy?"

"Why?" Terry stammered. It was the only word he could muster.

"So, you wish to know why I did what I did?" Silverman turned to face the window with only his profile in view to Terry. "Yes, I suppose I should tell you, but for you to understand, I must go back to the beginning. You see, my boy, I was never born with power like you were, nor blessed like my brother. No, I had to earn the strength I have now. Although I was born into a family of werewolves, I was never able to transform into one. Somehow the genes had skipped passed me. My parents were so ashamed that they locked me up in the basement. I was hidden from the public, to be ignored and forgotten. Imagine, a prisoner in my own home," said Silverman quietly. For a moment he remained silent and simply stared through the window at the scenery below.

"And yet," continued Silverman, his voice firm and clear, "somehow, my dear little brother was born blessed with extraordinary strength. Each night, my mother and father would sing his praises. How I hated it! I was their first born. I should have been their number one, but it was Beowulf who got everything that I deserved. I was entirely removed from their lives, save for the leftover meals brought to me on a tray once a night to ensure I was kept fed and alive. It drove me insane! What made him so special? I knew that if only I could prove my superiority, my parents would have to acknowledge me." Silverman sighed as if the memories had stirred a great sadness within. "But alas, that opportunity was taken from me on the night they were killed. With them gone, I was set free. Your father invited me to stay with him, but after years of watching him have everything I desired, the sight of him sickened me. I wanted to rip him to shreds, but I knew I lacked the power. Instead, I went my own way, seeking to study the genetics behind the werewolf mutation."

In between Silverman's speech, Terry could hear Fergus and Almira talking.

"Will he be okay?" said Fergus, looking at the wounds on the minotaur's chest.

"I think so," said Almira. "But I have to act fast."

Silverman ignored them and continued speaking. "Yet no matter where I went or what I did, my brother's shadow always followed me. News of his adventures and successes never left me alone … forever haunting me, taunting me," Silverman paused again, taking a deep breath and composing himself before continuing. "And then during a battle between the werewolves and the vampires, your father found himself infatuated with Elena Winter—a vampire—your mother. They escaped the battleground and were branded as traitors by their respective kinds." Silverman stepped away from the window to face Terry with the look of a cunning animal. His eyes narrowed into slits.

"They conceived you, but you were a sickly infant child—a half-breed—neither fully vampire nor wolf, and they had no one to turn to for help. Concerned for your health, your father sought me out. Imagine my surprise when I received a telegram from him asking for my help. Ha! The great Beowulf crying to his forgotten older brother. When I heard about you, I realised there and then that my prayers had been answered. There you were, my golden ticket to absolute power! A pure hybrid. I knew, at that moment, I needed to have you, and so I fashioned a brilliant plan to eliminate your parents and make you my own."

Silverman's eyes were now locked with Terry's. There was an almost insatiable thirst in his gaze as if he enjoyed delivering his revelation.

"You're mad," said Fergus as he stood next to Terry.

"I don't expect an empty skull to understand my brilliance," Silverman replied irritably.

180

Almira was still by Tompkins's side. She'd managed to close the wound on his chest using blue leaves, which she carried in one of her small belt pouches. The leaves had been placed over the wound to contain the blood flow and were held by some spell. By the look of relief on Almira's face, it seemed that the minotaur would pull through.

Silverman, however, didn't seem to care; he instead turned to the corpse of Mihai Winter and admired his handiwork. "Yes, it was a most intelligent plan, and it started when I approached your grandfather," said Silverman. "In his time, he was a well-known and powerful vampire. And of course, a grieving father concerned about his daughter's safety. I informed him that I knew of Elena's whereabouts, but I would only disclose the information to him on the condition that he killed Beowulf for me. Naturally, he agreed, the poor fool. So, I provided him with a place and a time." Silverman walked away from Winter, fixing his gaze on Terry once more. He smiled upon seeing Terry's clenched fists.

"What happened next?" said Terry, maintaining a steady voice despite the swelling anger that was building up inside.

"I leaked their whereabouts to the werewolves who wanted to capture Beowulf and Elena alive to hold a public execution for their marital crime, but I changed the time by five minutes to delay their arrival. With the preparations in place, I made my way to your birth home, a house in Cornwall. I approached your parents under the pretence of a regular health check-up, and whilst I tended to you in your room on the first floor, the doorbell rang, exactly on time. Just as I knew he would, Beowulf went down to answer, leaving your mother, Elena Winter, as the only obstacle in the room. As you may know, vampires are in a weakened state after giving birth due to the loss of blood and are unable to fend for themselves. I couldn't leave her as a witness or she would alert the others so I pierced her heart with a wooden stake and muffled her dying screams. I then grabbed you and made my escape through the back window."

A thunderous rumbling could be heard from afar, rain began pouring down, drumming against the windows.

"Y—you killed her? You killed my mother?" said Terry, his voice trembling as he spoke. No. No, this couldn't be true, he thought. His uncle had to be lying. He had to be.

A flash of lightning momentarily blinded everyone in the room.

"I imagine Mihai Winter once had the same dumbfounded look on his face as you now have," said Silverman calmly. "After killing Beowulf with a silver bullet, he must have been quite surprised to find an empty cradle and his daughter murdered. I assume he deduced that he'd been betrayed, but by then it was too late. The authorities arrived as scheduled."

"You were hoping they would do your dirty work for you and get rid of him?" said Terry.

"You're catching on. However, there was a small oversight on my part. I thought that the elite werewolf soldiers would be able to handle one measly aging vampire, and so I left, not bothering to check, but I was mistaken. It was to my great surprise when I learnt many years later from you, my boy, that your grandfather had survived. Needless to say, I wanted to finish the job. Of course, I could only do so thanks to the power I now have from you."

There was a wild, gleeful smile upon his face. It appeared almost manic and sent a shiver down Terry's spine.

"Ah!" said Silverman. "I see that you're wondering how. Naturally, I shall tell you. Although I never did spend much time with you, I did allow you to grow up freely for the most part. I had no desire to cage you in the same way I had been. Instead, I led you to believe that you were a day-walking vampire. Your werewolf half was supressed through medication to prevent outbreaks and drawing attention from neighbours."

Everything felt so jumbled and clear all at once. All the lies. All the deceit. His uncle had lied to him this entire time. He'd lied about everything. And he continued, unaware of Terry's realisations, only caring about telling his own version of the truth. With each word spoken, a vivid image planted itself in Terry's mind, and he felt sickened by what he'd heard.

"At the same time, I would take blood samples from you and experiment. During the course of my investigations, I kidnapped countless humans and monsters to use as guinea pigs and learn the secret of your power. Eventually, I succeeded, melding my own DNA with yours, allowing me to finally transform. Oh, how I relished my newfound power. But I had to test it ... I had to know just how powerful I really was. So, I frequented the monster world, utilising long forgotten portals and passageways. Once I had set up a base, I began terrorising these poor, pathetic creatures. Cornering unsuspecting monsters and sinking my claws into them."

"Innocent monsters," said Fergus. "You terrorised innocent monsters."

Silverman waved his hand in the air, unbothered. "There is no such thing as an innocent monster, boy. Regardless, I found myself dissatisfied, for there was no challenge. I could crush them all with ease, so instead, I started injecting my victims and forcing them to transform into half-wolves. At least, this way, they could put up a decent fight before I ripped them to shreds! Ha! It still wasn't enough! What good was being the most powerful creature if there was no one to challenge?" His voice dropped and he glared at Terry, his eyes penetrating his like a knife. "No one to prove my strength against?"

Terry shuddered, feeling his uncle's every word jolt into his bones.

Silverman sized up Terry with a predatory leer. "I realised my folly. I was still trapped in my brother's shadow. I couldn't move on. I still wanted to show my parents that I was the best. But Beowulf was dead, and so were my parents, so how could I ever demonstrate that I was superior? Then I had an idea, a brilliant spark. What if I could create a rival? An equal in power. And who better than the son of Beowulf? So, I thrust you into this new environment, my boy, allowing you to grow and mature, but by God, you've still a long way to go."

He had a mad glint in his eye that Terry had never seen before. Who was this stranger? Terry wondered.

Silverman licked his lips, "But perhaps you can give your uncle a small taster of what you've learned?"

"You're ... you're a monster," said Terry as he slowly backed away from him.

Silverman grinned with lascivious delight. "You know you look nothing like your father. I daresay you resemble your mother more than anything. I imagine that was who Mihai Winter saw when he caught sight of you. The man only wanted revenge and believed it was finally within his grasp. Poor soul never stood a chance. When you informed me that he was your teacher, I investigated his office. Unsurprisingly, I found a copy of your student records in his desk drawer and a map of the human world. It doesn't take a genius to deduce that he'd gone to our old home in search of me, so I returned to greet him. Oh, the surprise on his face when I revealed my hybrid form was truly something special. That's it! That's the look!" said Silverman, pointing a finger at Terry. "Keep it that way, won't you boy, while I tell you the rest of my story? Now, where was I? Ah yes …

"Winter underestimated me, a costly mistake. Unfortunately, I too, underestimated him. He managed to escape me, and although he'd lost a terrible amount of blood and was severely injured with lacerations across the chest, he'd somehow made it back to the island and was found by the headmistress. Lucky me, he passed out before he could mention my name. She, of course, got UGOM involved, which suffice to say, complicated matters for me. Winter's location was kept secret. Only select UGOM officials and the headmistress herself knew his whereabouts. And of course, the headmistress's trusted lapdog, Basil Tompkins."

Almira, crouching down by Tompkins's unconscious body, stood up to face Silverman with an expression of pure rage.

"Oh, have I hurt your feelings, princess?"

"You tricked him!"

"I tricked everyone, my dear. Tompkins believed he was helping a friend in need. By chance, I bumped into him when I returned to the island in search of Winter. Being the foolishly loyal minotaur that he is, he never revealed Winter's location, but he did offer me a temporary position as a substitute teacher. A perfect cover for my activities. Tompkins never suspected what I was up to until the last moment when I gave myself away by asking too many questions about Winter. It seems he went searching for my old lair and returned here to guard Winter when he couldn't find it, but as you can see, he failed miserably at that too."

"All of this just so you could fight Terry?" said Almira.

Silverman's entire body stiffened. "Have you any idea what it's like to spend your childhood waking up in a cold cellar, staring into a broken mirror just to prove to yourself that you still exist? I spent so long wondering why I was born so weak, but look at the power I've obtained," said Silverman, raising his palms. "I am an engine of destruction that can no longer be stopped. Yet, what good is all this power if there is no one for me to test it against? I crave a real challenge. The monsters in this world are pathetic shells of their former selves. I could snap them like twigs. So, I modelled you, my dear nephew, Terry, to be my equal. You're still to reach your peak, but I can no longer wait. With the two of you here, I may finally be able to go all out. Almira, descendant of the Khizaar, the most powerful of all the spellcasters. And my dear Terry, a hybrid formed from the monsters of legend—through your veins flows the blood of two of the greatest warriors in recent years. How I've thirsted for an opportunity like this."

"Um," said Fergus, butting in, "what about me? Aren't you going to acknowledge me? I'm here too, you know. Say something cool about me."

Silverman's bones moved under his skin and thick black hair sprouted all over his body as he increased in size, transforming from man to wolfpire. He lunged towards Terry, but before he had a chance to strike, Terry saw Almira mutter incantations as she waved her arms around madly. A heavy impact pushed Silverman backwards, causing him to tumble and fall. Shattering the window behind him as he fell through it, he crashed to the ground with a loud thud.

19

Restless Night

Almira dashed forward, leaping into the air to chase after Silverman.

"What is she thinking?" cried Fergus as he rushed past the broken glass and crouched down to see the sight below. He then turned his skull towards Terry. "We need to go after them."

"My uncle's a killer ... he's a killer ..." Terry whimpered as he stood frozen to the spot with an expression of shock and horror all over his face. "A monster."

The world he knew had been destroyed, and something inside him had broken.

A shadowy wolfish figure approached, and a hand beckoned Terry into the darkness.

"I'll swallow your despair, Terry Silverman."

A well of rage erupted from deep within him. All those years, his uncle had lied to him. For so long he'd been fooled, lulled into a false sense of family. No more. NO MORE! He surrendered control to the beast and jumped through the shattered window, leaving Fergus behind. He followed Almira and Silverman with only one desire in mind: to kill the monster.

Silverman's hairy wolfish body convulsed as he lay spread-eagled on the ground, and from his fanged jaw, a ferocious unearthly sound roared into the night. Crowds began to gather around him, screaming for help, not knowing whether to tend to him or run away from the angry thrashing beast.

Within a few moments, he'd hauled himself up and stumbled forwards in an attempt to strike Almira, who'd just reached the ground. The crowds dispersed in a frenzy, now shoving each other to get out of the away.

Almira moved swiftly, soaring into the air over Silverman and landing gracefully behind him. A sword materialised in her hand, and she twirled it briefly, as though to show off, and then swung it forward. Magic enhanced every muscle in her body, compensating for her small physique. There was a certain elegance to the way she moved, like a dancer. A deadly, magical, sword-wielding dancer.

Terry's wolfish alter ego grunted as he landed with a loud whoosh and sprang towards the battle. He leapt into the air with his furry hands out as he brought them down on Silverman, shredding his skin with his claws. Silverman let out an ear-splitting whine like the sound of a dog that had been lashed. The sheer force of Almira and Terry's combined attack had the monster writhing in agony as he shielded his eyes with his large hairy hands. But before Terry knew it, he was being forced back with brute force and slammed to the ground.

Almira shot up into the air and swung her sword towards Silverman's head, but he dodged and knocked the weapon out her hand. A second later, she was sent hurtling into the distance.

Then to Terry's surprise, he saw Fergus rushing towards the beast. He had no idea how the clanking skeleton had gotten down so quickly, but he was relieved to see him.

Fergus grabbed a handful of pebbles and flung them at Silverman in a futile attempt to divert his attention. "Leave my friends alone!" he yelled. The monster brushed him aside with a single swipe, smashing the skeleton apart as his bones went flying.

Seeing his friends struck down flooded Terry with fury. He jumped up and sunk his fanged teeth into Silverman's hairy shoulder, drawing blood. Silverman howled in response and thrust his claws into Terry's abdomen, piercing into his flesh.

Terry released and bellowed in pain. He hammered his head against Silverman's, causing the monster to temporarily lose focus. Taking advantage of Silverman's confusion, Terry grabbed Silverman's beastlike hand wrenching the claws free from his stomach. Terry smacked him across his jaw, forcing the beast to stumble, but Silverman felt a renewed volcanic strength. He held his ground and struck back. Several heavy hits pummelled Terry in succession, and he found himself being picked up and thrown through the air like a ragdoll. *THUMP! BANG! CRASH!* This was not going well for him. He lay on the ground, spluttering out blood before he picked himself up, standing strong once more.

"Marvellous!" cried Silverman, applauding as he walked towards Terry. "Truly marvellous! A normal vampire or werewolf would have been knocked out from such a ferocious fight as this, but here you are, strong as ever and raring to go!"

Terry couldn't believe how different his uncle's voice was. It was deep and guttural, as if every word echoed into the distance, nothing like the man he had known. No, he couldn't think like that anymore. Whatever delusions he'd had about his uncle had to be stored away if he was to stand a chance against the beast now standing before him. He braced himself, wiping the sweat from his forehead as he threw his shoulders back.

Silverman wiped the saliva from his mouth with the back of his hand and began to pick up pace, charging towards Terry.

Terry roared and lunged forward, attempting to deliver a strike, but was instead greeted by a series of successive counterattacks as his opponent's claws slashed into his hair covered skin, drawing blood. He doubled over, panting with exhaustion, feeling overpowered by the older and much larger Silverman, no longer able to defend himself. And although his wolfpire form provided him with instant healing, he could still feel the impact of each strike, and his stamina was slowly draining away. He stepped backwards, attempting to create distance, but Silverman quickly closed in again and dealt a heavy blow that sent Terry crashing into a building.

His face contorted. There was a searing pain in his left side. Ugh, was this it? Was this the extent of his training? Something sharp had been lodged into his stomach. He attempted to get up, but his body would no longer respond.

The screams of creatures in the crowds began to ring in his ears and his vision blurred. He could just about make out the figure of Silverman approaching, and he knew he had to move, but he could feel himself slipping into darkness. He needed a moment to rest, a moment to reset … just a moment.

***

Terry looked around, he seemed to be standing back at the fair in his normal form. The festival lights burned intensely; he was surrounded by shadowy, unrecognisable figures moving slowly in a ghostly manner—hovering and paying no attention to him. What was he doing here? Wasn't Terry in the middle of something? But he couldn't remember what. He rubbed his forehead. Think, Terry. Something was wrong, but he couldn't place his finger on it. He glanced down at his body. No cuts, no bruises. Why was he checking for injuries?

Almira appeared next to him and locked arms with Terry. "Come on, it'll be fun," she said with a bright smile.

"Where are we going?" asked Terry, confused.

"Where else, but the funhouse," said Almira. She pointed to a large unsightly demonic werewolf head, a creature of nightmares. Terry didn't wish to venture any further, but Almira pulled him through the wide-open

194

mouth, and he became lost in a hall of mirrors. In each reflection was a scared, distorted child reaching out to him.

Suddenly, one of the mirrors shattered and a strong hand grabbed Terry by the throat, holding him up. His legs swinging freely, he gasped for air, struggling for freedom.

The Demon Wolf snarled and threw Terry to the ground. He stood on hind legs, looming over Terry, his presence threatening.

Between them stepped Almira, holding out both her arms each side. The monster lunged at her, his claws piercing through her stomach, and she bent over, spluttering out blood.

"ALMIRA!" cried Terry.

The monster pulled her up with a single hand and threw her aside. Her body slammed against a mirror, and she fell onto the shattered glass. More concerned about his friend than the monster, Terry tried shaking her. "Almira! Get up, Almira! No, no, no, no, no." He pulled her close to him, holding her tightly. "Please, Almira, I need you. I can't do this without you."

"You're weak, Terry Silverman," said the Demon Wolf.

Terry cast a backward glance, his eyes widening in shock. In the creature's hand was Fergus's skull.

"You can't protect your friends. You can't even protect yourself," said the monster, crushing the skull and turning it to dust in his palm.

"I'LL KILL YOU!" Terry roared, and in an instant, he was silenced. Blood splattered onto the floor where his heart had been pierced by the monster's claws. Terry fell to his knees and onto the cold floor. The world came to a stop and he was blanketed in darkness.

***

"Terry!" cried a voice. "Terry!"

Terry's eyes opened. He was no longer at the festival, no longer dreaming. Instead, he was in the middle of the forest, resting against a tree, and crouched next to him was Fergus, with both his bony hands on Terry's shoulders.

"You okay?" said Fergus, taking his hands off Terry. "You looked like you were having a nightmare."

Terry placed his hand over his chest and waited for his heartbeat to steady. He allowed himself a moment to enjoy the cool air. It was peaceful, and the only sound he could hear was the wind howling. No, that wasn't quite right. There was something in the distance, the sounds of someone shouting and an otherworldly howling.

"Where's Almira and my uncle?" Terry demanded. He tried to sit up, but felt a sharp pain and winced, slipping back down.

"Easy there, they're still fighting," said Fergus. "They're not far from here."

"Why are we in the forest?"

"Almira cast a spell to bring the fight here. I think she wanted to give you time to recover and possibly also protect any bystanders from getting hurt, but I'm worried her magic is now severely drained. I don't think she'll last much longer."

Terry watched the leaves fall from the branches as they whirled around in the wind, and as the full moon peeked into view from behind a cloud, Terry stared right at it. "How could he do it, Fergus? How could he kill my parents and lie to me all these years?" Terry tried hiding his pain, but even he could hear his own voice crack. It was like a heavy anchor weighing down on his chest. He wiped away his tears with his hand and turned his face towards Fergus.

Fergus placed a comforting bony hand on Terry's shoulder. For a while, neither of them said a word and simply sat in silence, listening to the wind wailing in the night.

"I'm afraid," Terry whispered. "What if I'm not strong enough to beat him?"

"It's fine if you're weaker," said Fergus gazing at him. "We just need to outsmart him."

20

The Witch's Apprentice

As he ran towards the battle, Terry was soon able to see Silverman desperately trying to slice Almira up with his claws and her dodging as best as she could, just barely escaping any lethal attacks. She managed to create some distance between herself and the beast and held up a hand as if to ward Silverman back. She then chanted a quick incantation. Three magic circles materialised from her palm, one after another, each circle larger than the next. Through the centre of each circle, a green energy beam fired out like a bullet, piercing into Silverman's right leg. She fired several more bullets in succession, each cutting through the monster's flesh, causing him to scream out and stumble around as if he could barely hold himself up. The magic circles shattered, and Almira lowered her hand. She was breathing heavily, the strain of using ongoing magic on a large scale must have taken its toll on her.

Silverman grunted and dropped to his knees, punching his fist against the ground. Blood dripped from the wounds on his leg from Almira's attack, but he remained strong, his wounds now closing and healing. He shot up, charging forwards towards Almira. She dodged the attack by leaping out the way, but Silverman managed to grab her by her boots and sent her flying into the forest. She disappeared from sight only to reappear almost instantly holding daggers in each hand. Rushing at Silverman, she stabbed his legs as he howled in pain, and in return, he lashed out, grabbing her and then throwing her down. She no longer had the strength to stand. Silverman grinned. He raised his blood-drenched claws and brought them down in an attempt to end the spellcaster's life, but then found his bulky frame being pushed sideways.

In his wolfish form, Terry had pinned Silverman onto the ground and bared his fangs at the monster.

"Well, well, well, back for more, are we?" said Silverman. He thrust his lower body upwards and shoved Terry off.

They both got up and now circled each other.

Terry glared at Silverman, his teeth gritted. "You'll pay for this. I won't let you lay another finger on her."

Silverman rolled his eyes. "Please, spare me the generic threats," he said calmly. "We both know you can't beat me. You've already tried and failed, rather miserably, I might add. You know I'm so disappointed! I was expecting at least somewhat of a challenge."

Terry used his right clawed foot to strike Silverman's left leg, catching him off-balance. As the monster fell, Terry sunk his fanged teeth into Silverman's shoulder and ripped out a lump of flesh, which he spat to the side as he watched the beast writhe in agony on the ground.

Silverman remained still for a moment as if processing what had just happened. He picked himself up, his body repairing and healing itself as he did. He saw Terry had reverted to his normal form and cocked his head. "Giving up?" he asked.

Terry didn't respond.

Silverman opened his jaws and tried biting into Terry, but Terry sidestepped out of the way and moved in for another attack, quickly transforming again and knocking Silverman back several feet before reverting to his normal self.

"Curious," said Silverman, rubbing his jaw. He sprung forward, attempting to take Terry down, but found himself outmanoeuvred at every turn.

Terry constantly reverted back and forth from his wolfpire form to dodge and counterattack, leaving Silverman unable to land a single strike. Terry had tried fighting this way with Almira during his training, but against her, he'd only managed to gain a temporary advantage. Almira was far quicker and more agile than him, and she was able to adapt her own form flitting up, down, and sideways as he morphed from beast to vampire. However, against Silverman, who was much bigger and slower by comparison, it was proving far more effective. His size made it difficult for him to hit the ever-changing proportions of Terry's body.

Yes! Terry's confidence was rising. His body still ached all over, and each move made him wince in even greater pain than the last, so he knew he wouldn't last much longer in this state. But for the first time, he finally felt as if he had a shot at winning. He moved behind Silverman and grabbed him, holding him steady. "Now!" Terry yelled.

Fergus took the cue and charged forward, holding the silverwood stake like a spear. He stabbed a surprised Silverman through the chest as Silverman howled in pain and broke free from Terry's grip, knocking both Terry and Fergus down.

Silverman grabbed the stake with both clawed hands and pulled it out, breathing heavily. "What an interesting item you have here," he said, inspecting the relic before snapping it in half and dropping it to the ground. "Whatever it was, too bad it didn't work, eh?"

Terry's insides churned. He looked down and realised Silverman had sunk his claws into his gut. Before he could retaliate, he was dealt with another attack. Then several more followed in sequence, Silverman's claws cutting into Terry's hairy chest, tearing at the flesh. Silverman lifted Terry up and sent him hurling and smashing into a tree. He laid on the ground, trying to piece together what had just happened. His moment of victory had been short lived. How foolish he was to think he could beat the legendary Demon Wolf. He could hear his heartbeat drumming in his ears and warm blood filled his mouth.

Silverman approached him, his breath in ragged gasps. He loomed over Terry but no longer looked so frightening. "Was this … the best … you could do?" he said, wiping the blood from his mouth. Then his hand shot up, gripping his chest where the stake had pierced him. "Almira taught you well. Your parents would be proud."

Terry felt a fresh rush of rage overwhelm him. With his newfound strength, he hauled himself up, his face contorted with the flare of pain, and he delivered a powerful strike to Silverman that made the monster collapse. Terry buried him in vicious blows over and over again. This was the man that had led him to believe he loved him, the man who'd killed his parents and stolen his childhood from him. If it weren't for him, Terry would still have both his parents and been part of a family who cherished him. He would have known what it was like to wait for a father to pick him up from school instead of walking home alone on a cold wintery night. He would have known what it would be like to feel the warm embrace of a mother when the world felt like it was going to crumble. He would have known what it would be like to truly be loved. He roared in fury. All he could feel now was Silverman's bones crack as his face became swollen and unrecognisable as his uncle gasped for breath.

"Enough!" said Fergus, his shaking hand grabbing Terry's shoulder. "Enough," he repeated. "It's over."

Terry paused, seeing his own blood-drenched hands, and reverted back to his normal form. He looked at the bloodied face of his uncle. Why did it have to turn out this way? Here was someone Terry had loved all his life, and in spite of everything he'd done to him, a part of him still cared for the man.

As if Brian Silverman could tell exactly what Terry's thoughts were, the old man spoke in a soft, weak voice. "If only you could have seen the world as I had seen it," he paused, his breathing slowing. "Then perhaps you would have understood. Can you hear the hollow rasps of my breath? That's my life, leaving me. Whatever I was impaled with did the trick. Time has not been kind to my mind, and the sand in the hourglass is now nearly gone."

When Terry needed them most, no words came to him, only tears.

Silverman raised his hand like a feeble old man and Terry held it firmly.

"Do not burden your soul, my boy. For what it is worth, I am sorry. Heh, how amusing, that only in the light of death all darkness is uncovered."

"Step away from the beast," commanded a bulky, unfriendly looking goblin dressed in black armour and holding a large battle axe. On the goblin's chest plate were the words UGOM printed in yellow, and behind him were many more similar looking goblins.

Terry looked back at Silverman and stared into his uncle's eyes one last time before finally standing up and stepping away.

Several of UGOM's goblins came forward and tied the creature's hands and legs with chains and placed a bite restraint muzzle onto the beast before carrying the monster away.

21

From Myth to Legend

As the days went by, Fergus Gravestone became incredibly popular. Rumours spread about his bravery against the Demon Wolf and how he'd fearlessly slayed the monster with a silver stake through the heart. The media were eating him up, calling him the 'Skull Master', a nickname that made no sense to Terry. He'd been interviewed multiple times by reporters and had received a large number of thank you letters from the public.

"Look! Look! It's him!" people would shout as he walked by. "The one who slayed the Demon Wolf! The Skull Master!"

"That's the one!" another yelled.

"He's so handsome!"

"This is like a dream come true," said Fergus, putting down the newspaper which had headlines of his so-called heroics. "Can you believe they'll be awarding me with a trophy tomorrow night for my bravery? What am I going to say? I'll need to prepare a speech. Oh, don't worry, Terry, you're mentioned here too. Maybe they'll award you with a trophy as well. It'll probably be smaller than mine though. After all, I am the legendary hero."

A group of students and a few teachers were waiting excitedly outside the classroom as Terry and Fergus approached them in the hallway. This was the fourth night in a row that small crowds of fans gathered before the start of registration.

Terry sighed. "Not again."

"Skull Master! Skull Master! Can I get an autograph?" said an energetic young elf, holding up a pen and notebook for Fergus to sign. The rest followed suit and clamoured around the skeleton.

"Please! There's enough of me to go around!" said Fergus, taking the pen from the elf first. "Now, who should I make this one out to?"

Terry shook his head and headed for the door but stopped when he noticed Almira at the other end of the hallway. She was wearing a cast around her right arm and had several cuts all over her but smiled the moment Terry approached her.

"How are you holding up?" asked Terry.

"Oh this?" said Almira, pointing at the cast with her free hand. "Nothing to worry about. I may not be able to heal as fast as you, but I'll be fine. More importantly, what about you? I'm surprised you didn't take a few nights off with all that's happened."

"I'm fine," said Terry. "I think … I don't know. I just need to keep busy."

"Your call. How are the interrogations going?"

Each night since the incident, a government officer had dropped by to ask Terry questions regarding his involvement, and each time it was a different officer. Terry always kept to the same story. He never mentioned that he could transform nor that the Demon Wolf was his uncle. For whatever reason, when Silverman died, he remained in his wolfpire form, and there seemed to be no records of his existence for UGOM to identify him. All Terry mentioned was how he helped distract the beast in the forest to give the Skull Master enough time to slay him.

"I've only told them what you told me to say. Nothing more. Nothing less."

"Good," said Almira. "We need to keep our story consistent."

"It would've been more believable to say you beat him," said Terry.

Almira shrugged. "I don't care much for the attention. Besides, it wouldn't work anyway since I was knocked out when UGOM's goblins arrived."

"How's Tompkins doing?"

"He's good. He should be out of the hospital tomorrow night in time for the Skull Master's award ceremony. I'm going to pay him a visit later tonight. You want to come?"

Terry stared at his feet. "I don't know. I feel like a hypocrite for not trusting him because of his appearance. In the human realm, people often didn't trust me and feared me because of the way I looked, and here I come to this realm and do the same to Tompkins."

"Hey," said Almira, placing her free hand on Terry's shoulder and squeezing it. "At least you've realised your mistake. Now the only question is have you learned from it?"

She always seemed to know what to say, thought Terry, looking into her blue eyes. "Thank you," he whispered.

"What for?" said Almira.

"Everything. I never said this to anyone, but on my first night here, I dreamt about you. I was falling from the skies, but you flew in on your broom and saved me. I thought it was just a silly dream, something I forgot for a while. Turns out, it held more meaning than I thought. You saved me, and I don't know how I can repay you."

Almira smiled. "You don't need to thank me or repay me. I'll always be around to help." She turned round, and as she left, she said, "You know where to find me if you ever need me."

***

Later on, in the middle of class, Terry's name was called out by an UGOM official. He was a giant with a thick moustache and curly brown hair. And he dressed like he was on holiday at a beach, wearing shorts and sunglasses.

"Nice to meet you, I'm Hans Coil," he said, offering Terry a handshake.

Terry returned the gesture.

"I'm here on UGOM business," explained Hans Coil. "I'll need you to come with me."

Terry rolled his eyes. He expected this interrogation to be completed the same way as the rest, but when he reached the headmistress's office, he realised this time might be different.

Inside, the headless headmistress was standing by her desk. Instead, seated in her seat was a tall thin man with jelled jet-black hair, bony arms, and a pale complexion.

"Greetings, I am Snark Dia, the Prime President of UGOM," said the man as he stood up and shook hands with Terry. "Take a seat," he instructed, gesturing Terry to the chair before seating himself. "I have a few questions for you. Hans, close the door."

Hans Coil did as instructed and stood by the door with his arms folded.

"Now Terry," began Snark Dia, tapping his fingers together. "I'd like to ask you about the incident at the Halloween festival with the Demon Wolf."

"I've already told UGOM everything I know," said Terry.

"Have you now?" Snark Dia eyed Terry, carefully studying his expression.

"Yeah, I have," replied Terry calmly.

"Some of the eyewitnesses claim that they saw a second Demon Wolf at the festival. Can you tell me anything about that?"

Terry shrugged his shoulders. "No idea."

"I can understand why the spellcaster and the Skull Master were in the forest, but can you tell me what you were doing there?"

"I got caught in their transportation spell."

"And yet you never saw the second Demon Wolf?"

"It's all a blur, sir. I was too scared to really pay attention."

Snark Dia remained silent for some time and simply kept tapping his fingers together, calculating his next words.

"Your friend, the now famous Skull Master, defeated one Demon Wolf, but he let the other get away."

"Killing one alone is pretty impressive if you ask me, sir."

"I find it difficult to believe that a skeleton could defeat the Demon Wolf alone. Unless he was being assisted by a friend?"

"Yes, a friend like the spellcaster who also fought the Demon Wolf. I know she got knocked out, but she did weaken the creature before that happened. That allowed for the Skull Master to take him."

"Deflection. Clever," said Snark. "I see you've thought this through."

"Not sure what you mean, sir. I'm just telling the truth."

"Or a version of it. I find it strange that in all the reports, you've remembered a great amount of detail, and yet you've no memory of the second Demon Wolf."

Terry didn't say anything, and they remained in silence for a while.

"My, my," said Snark Dia, finally. "I suspect you have a skeleton in your closet, Terry Silverman."

He had no idea, thought Terry, thinking about the literal skeleton sleeping in his closet.

Snark Dia shot a brief glance at the headmistress who remained still and expressionless. "Very well, Terry, you may leave."

Terry nodded and made his way to the door.

"Oh, one last request," said Snark Dia. "Could you send in the Skull Master for me? I'd just love for a chance to meet the legendary hero who slayed the Demon Wolf and saved us."

"No problem, but I have to warn you, sir," said Terry. "He can be a bit of a handful."

22

Between Love and Hate

The awards ceremony was held in the assembly hall. It was packed full of not only students and teachers, but also the local media and residents from the town of Grimdale—all of them wanting to honour the hero who'd saved them from the Demon Wolf.

Terry was seated towards the back of the hall with the rest of House Carmilla. Fergus was nowhere in sight. The skeleton had gone on ahead before Terry, leaving him without anyone he knew well enough to sit next to. He did initially consider sitting next to Emmy, but he noticed Kurt staring at the time, so he didn't bother. It was a shame that Almira was in a different house or he'd have sat next to her—fittingly for her though, she was in House Arsalan.

At the front of the stage, positioned at the stand, was the headless headmistress with a gold skull shaped trophy in hand. Standing next to her was the minotaur, Basil Tompkins, who appeared to be back to full health. Behind him, seated on chairs, were the teachers of Grimerth and some other creatures that Terry did not recognise, with the exception of one, Hans Coil, who appeared completely uninterested.

"Ahem! The headmistress would like to thank everyone for their attendance here tonight," said Tompkins, on behalf of the headless woman. "For too long, we've lived in fear, afraid of becoming victims of the Demon Wolf, but no more. Now we've finally returned to safety and it's all thanks to the bravery of an individual who I'm sure needs no introduction. Fellow monsters, please give a warm round of applause for the one, the only, the Skull Master!"

All of a sudden, loud, adrenaline pumping music started playing, and Fergus Gravestone stepped out onto the stage from behind the drawn curtains dressed in purple robes and wearing a shoulder bag. He pointed his bony fingers at the crowd, and the audience roared with excitement, clapping and crying out his name.

"I love you, Skull Master!" yelled one of the students.

Terry couldn't help but smile a little. He knew how happy the skeleton must be right now. Fergus had been so excited about tonight that he'd actually woken up early for once and bothered putting on clothes to make himself look presentable in front of everyone.

"Thank you! Thank you!" said Fergus as the music died down. "You're too kind!" He shook hands with Tompkins and then the headless headmistress before accepting the trophy and taking the stand. "You know, I've always wondered what it would be like to be loved and adored by others. I have to say, it really is an incredible feeling." He took a moment to admire the skull shaped trophy. "I'm so overwhelmed by this award that I could just cry, but since I'm only bones, that would be very difficult, now wouldn't it?"

The audience laughed at his terrible joke.

"But seriously folks," continued Fergus, "there are two reasons why I was successful in my victory against the evil Demon Wolf, and I'd like to take a moment to thank them both."

He reached into his shoulder bag, putting away his trophy, and then pulled out a crumpled up piece of paper and some glasses. He put on the glasses and placed the piece of paper on the stand. Then he reached back into his bag and pulled out something very small which he held up, it was difficult to make out what though.

"The first is this pebble which I used to distract the Demon Wolf, drawing him away from the innocent monsters of Grimdale."

Fergus put the pebble back in the bag and reached in for something else.

Terry couldn't see the next item from where he was seated, but he knew it must be the silverwood stake that had been snapped in two.

"And then there's this silverwood stake, which I used to stab the creature's heart."

Yup, he was right, thought Terry.

Fergus set the broken stake down on the stand and picked up his crumpled piece of paper to read from. "Now, traditionally this relic is used to slay hybrids, but in this instance, I had this stake imbued with magical properties which have evaporated now. Unfortunately, if anyone wanted to test this, they couldn't. That said, my esteemed colleague Almira, can vouch for this."

A couple of people exchanged confused glances, but other than that, the assembly was dead silent. Terry couldn't tell if anyone was actually taking Fergus seriously or not. He tried glancing in Almira's direction to see her reaction, but her face was turned away and staring at the floor. If Terry had to guess, she was probably embarrassed.

"Anyway," continued Fergus. "It was a powerful spell for slaying demons which the Demon Wolf was foolish to overlook, for to a demon a monster is nothing. Ha, a costly mistake."

Fergus put the paper down and tapped his skull with a bony finger. "It was with this cunning of intellect that I was able to put the demon to rest. So, let this be a lesson to any who dare threaten us again, a warning to those who think we can be trampled on because of our kind nature. We may be nice, but step on us and we will fight back."

With that, Fergus removed his glasses, bowed his head and stepped down from the stand; as he did, the audience exploded the hall with a loud round of applause and cheers.

"Thank you for that, err, lovely speech," said Tompkins, as the headless headmistress returned to the stand. "To mark this great occasion, UGOM have decreed that henceforth, the first working night of November shall be a public night off for all and forever be remembered as Gravestone Night."

And an even louder applause than before followed.

***

Fergus and the rest of the school were busy celebrating that night. Terry, however, sat alone outside the castle at the bottom of the steep stone steps that led to the entrance. He sighed, looking down at the dirt on the ground and feeling the wind brush against his cheeks. He could hear the sound of someone walking down the steps, but he didn't bother to check who it was.

"So, this is where you were," said Tompkins.

"I wasn't really in the mood of celebrating," said Terry.

"That's understandable." The minotaur sat down next to Terry.

"How are you feeling?" said Terry.

"Well, thank you. Almira's quick attention saved me from spending months in recovery."

"She always seems to know what to do."

"I wouldn't say always." Tompkins reached into the inner breast pocket of his suit. "I have something for you." He pulled out a white envelope, which he then handed to Terry.

"What's this?" asked Terry, taking the envelope.

"I found it in Mihai Winter's office," said Tompkins. "Open it."

Terry tore open the envelope with his pointed nails and found a letter inside from his uncle, which he immediately read.

My dear boy,

I suppose this means that you've won our little scuffle and that I am no more of this world. In life, there are almost no guarantees, and though I try to account for all possibilities, the greatest one I could never account for were my feelings for you.

For so long, I loved no one. You were the only family I had left, and as I watched you grow, I found myself, for the first time in my life, actually caring for someone else. You gave me purpose and hope. Hope that I could finally have a worthy adversary. I longed to see you in all your glory and put my strength to the test.

The fact that you are reading this is proof that you did not disappoint. I am proud of you, my boy. Hold your head up high, and do what I could not, let the past go and move forward.

Ever yours,
Brian Silverman

Terry rubbed his eyes after reading the letter, holding back his tears. Tompkins was still sitting beside him, steam exhaling from his snout.

"Almira told me your uncle's story," said Tompkins. "How he was made to feel useless all his life, unwanted by his parents, and the jealously he felt for his brother, which in turn gave birth to his lust for murder and power so that he could, at last, be recognised for something. I only wish I could have realised sooner and stopped him."

They continued to sit in silence for a moment, a single leaf whirled around in the wind.

Then Tompkins spoke again. "Sometimes, the line between love and hate can be a little unclear. Despite everything your uncle did, I believe that in his own way, he truly did love you."

"What happens to me now?" said Terry. With his uncle gone, he had no legal guardian to take care of him, and once his allowance ran out, he'd have no money left either.

"You'll stay with us," said Tompkins.

"Us?" questioned Terry, looking up and into the minotaur's white slits.

"Myself and Almira. I bet she never told you, but she's been under my care for some time. Did you think you were the only orphan?"

There was a lump in Terry's throat. How could he ever have suspected such a nice person just because of the way they looked? He felt so ashamed of himself, throwing his arms around the minotaur and letting all the tears he'd been holding back finally spill out. And when Tompkins placed his hand on Terry's back, he knew that everything would be okay.

Acknowledgments

I'd like to thank my good friend, Nicholas Smith, for helping me brainstorm, reading each draft, and tightening dialogue. To Sherron Mayes and Nicole Boccelli, thank you both for your superb editing and proofreading. To Jennifer Birgersson, thank you for gifting me with your wonderful art.

Thank you to Sarah Mae, Jade Addis-McGlasham, Julie Smith, Jacqueline Canning, Caitlyn Huehn, Megan Manzano, Bhavina Vadgama, Philip Womack, Maddy Drake, and Idris Cheikh for the feedback and insight provided in the earlier drafts of the story.

Thank you to my parents and my siblings for the support you've all provided me.

And to you, my reader, thank you for following Terry on his journey. I hope you've enjoyed this story. If you have, please leave a short review on Amazon or on Goodreads. Both Terry and I would really appreciate it.

Terry Silverman

Half vampire. Half werewolf. All vegetarian. He can often be found with a carton of tomato juice in his hand. He likes movies and books about monsters and aliens.

Almira Khizaar

She loves fighting. She's trained in hand-to-hand combat, so don't mess with her. Seriously, don't. You'll regret it. She could probably snap you in two.

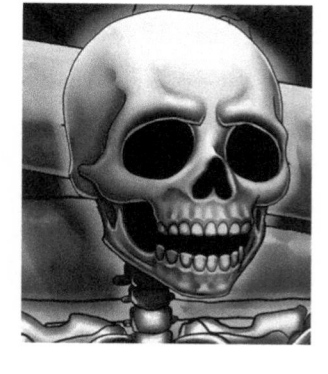

The Skull Master

A living legend, his bravery unparalleled. Evil trembles at the mere mention of his name. Beware the Skull Master. Beware his power. The strongest of the monsters. Defeat is not in his dictionary.

The Seal of the Khizaar

User of this magic beware, this is a spell only for those
who share my blood. With it comes strength and power.
Power of the Spellcaster for the Ages. And for those who
dare defy, a terrible price you will pay.

Sign up to be notified of new releases by visiting
www.spellcraftpress.com